The front door shattered inward. Her mouth opened for a scream, but there was no sound. Shards of glass tumbled end over end across the carpeting, tinkled on the tables like wind chimes. She tried to duck away from the knifelike missiles, but they struck her mercilessly, and still the glass rained in from the door.

And there was no wind.

Finally, the scream found its way out, and she pressed her bleeding hands to her face to protect her eyes. She tripped and nearly lost consciousness when her hands struck the floor and drove the glass deeper into her skin.

She was going to bleed to death. She was going to die slowly under a shroud of drifting pink. . . .

The HOUR OF THE OXRUN DEAD

When it strikes, you'll shudder!

Look for all these Tor books by Charles L. Grant

AFTER MIDNIGHT (Editor)
GREYSTONE BAY (Editor)
THE HOUR OF THE OXRUN DEAD
MIDNIGHT (Editor)
NIGHTMARE SEASONS (Editor)
THE ORCHARD

The HOUR OF THE OXRUN DEAD

CHARLES L. GRANT

A TOM DOHERTY ASSOCIATES BOOK

THE HOUR OF THE OXRUN DEAD

Copyright © 1987 by Charles L. Grant

First Tor printing: February 1987

A TOR Book

Published by Tom Doherty Associates, Inc.
49 West 24 Street
New York, N.Y. 10010

Cover art by David Mann

ISBN: 0-812-51862-4
CAN. ED.: 0-812-51863-2

Printed in the United States of America

0 9 8 7 6 5 4 3 2 1

Author's Dedication

For Beauty Light and Beauty Dark,
For faith, and believing,
And loving the things that go bump in the night:
For Karen who smiles, and Sharon who laughs,
Oxrun's my home and they're welcome any time.

Chapter 1

THE WANING moon spread a worn blanket of pale silver across the center of the room's darkness. It was an impersonal glow that bleached the lines from Natalie's face and replaced them with grey shadows, creating pits and hollows to give her the look of a freshly unearthed skull.

Her quilt, its rills deepened to indigo, had bunched at her neck, and its faded satin edging pushed up over her chin. She shivered once, and her legs grew taut, relaxed, and her knees inched slowly toward her chest. Suddenly she jerked them straight and twisted sharply on her side. A hand shoved the quilt impatiently to her waist, then pressed itself against her ear as if the thin fingers could filter the voices out of the silent room.

One Alpha, this is Control, over. One Alpha, this is Control.

Control, One Alpha here. What have you got for me now, Sammy? A robbery of the Park Street Bank, I hope.

Don't you wish, Dick Tracy. No, I got a call here from a Mrs. Leonard Jamieson at 1176 High Street. She says there's a prowler in her back yard.

What? At four in the morning? What's she been drinking, for crying out loud? And for how long?

Ben—

And what in heaven's name is she doing up so late? Doesn't she know what time it is?

Ben—

For crying out loud, Sammy!

Ben, all I do is get them and call them. I don't run a contest for their originality or time telling.

All right, Sammy, all right. I'm on my way. And thanks for tagging me. We certainly wouldn't want to wake the others, would we?

Roger, One Alpha, and call on your arrival.

Roger, Control.

And keep your comments to yourself.

Natalie thrust the hand away from her head and groped blindly for the quilt. Failing to find it, she drew up one leg, kicked and pushed the tufted wool onto the bare floor.

The sudden chill on her legs disturbed but did not interrupt an already precarious sleep; the hand returned to her ear.

A tangled strand of dark hair slipped into her mouth, then, as she rolled her face away from the window, her tongue worked, pushed out the hair, licked at full lips that hinted at black in the grey light. She sighed. Pressed her fingers tighter against her skull. Shuddering.

Control, this is One Alpha.

One Alpha, roger. A bit of static but I hear you good, Ben.

Your English is lousy, Sam, do you know that? And so's your sense of direction. Did you say 1176 High?

That's right, Ben. You there now?

Well, sure I'm here. Where else would I be at this time of night? And I've got news for you, brother. This here house is locked up tight. There's a garage door open, but there's no car inside. I already took a quick look around, and even the stupid crickets are sleeping. For crying out loud.

You ring the bell?

At four o'clock in the morning? Are you nuts? I knocked front and back, but no one answered. The shades are up, no curtains that I can see. Grass needs cutting badly, too. There just ain't nobody home, Sam. There ain't nobody home at all.

Can't be. I got the call.

You want me to go in or something?

Wait one. Let me think a minute.

Oh, brother!

Perspiration trembled into droplets in the shallows of her temples, the sides of her nose, under her lower lip. She threw an arm over her eyes, and her breasts heaved once against her flannel nightgown. The fingers of her left hand clenched, opened, fumbled and gripped the edge of the mattress. Her teeth began to chatter. Another sigh that lingered before whirling into a choking gasp.

Ben, check the mail box. Look for a name or something.

Wait one, slave driver ... Sam? There is none, believe it or not. Just a hole where the post used to be. I went onto the porch again, and there are a couple of broken windows on the first floor. They have tar paper tacked over them. Didn't see that the first time. Sam, I hate to tell you this, but this place is deserted. Nobody's lived here for a good long time.

What? A joke. It must be a stupid practical joke.

At four in the morning?

Ben, do you have to keep saying that?

Absolutely! Nat's probably listening in and I want her to go back to bed. Now!

Ben, you've been told before we don't allow personal messages over the radio. You're going to get nabbed for that one of these days.

So I'll never make Chief. Big deal, who needs it? And if it'll make you happy, I'll never do it again.

Fine.

Just as long as Nat goes to bed.

Ben!

The gasp caught in her throat, bubbled as though she were gargling. She coughed twice, and her fingers trailed to the floor, touched wood and recoiled, moving quickly to her stomach where they fisted and she rubbed tight circles over her glistening skin.

Ben, you might as well hit the road. I'll leave a note for the day shift to check on the—

Hold it, Sam! I've got the spotlight down the side of the house. I think I saw something in the back yard. I just got a glimpse. It ... cat ... big thing, it looks ... do you say?

Hold it, Ben. There's a ton of static on the wire. I can hardly understand what you're saying. I don't want you to be a hero. Stick by the car until I call Moss and—

My God! Did you see that?

Ben, for crying out loud, if the captain should hear that kind of talk you'll be back on the park beat.

Sam, if that's what I think it . . . can't be . . . promised . . . wait a minute, the cord's caught on the steering . . . getting out for a closer . . . Sam, did you—

Ben, not on the radio!

Don't believe it. It isn't . . . have to shoot, Sam . . . oh, my God! . . . promised, he promised . . . oh, my God, Sam!

Ben? Benny? One Alpha, this is Control, over. One Alpha, this is Control. Ben? Confound it, Ben, talk to me! . . . Two Alpha, this is Control. Haul over to 1176 High ASAP. Ben's in some kind of trouble. Move! . . . One Alpha, this is Control, over.

Control, this is Two Alpha. What's all the shouting?

Moss, if you'd been monitoring like you're supposed to instead of—never mind, just get over to 1176 High and see if you can make some sense out of what's going on there. Ben's in trouble, I think. Move!

The noise finally escaped her throat and dipped into a whimper, a choked-off scream, and Natalie sat up abruptly, her mouth wide to gulp at the chilled air and fill the gaps in

her lungs. She blinked against the moonlight, and as the stiffness in her back faded,
one hand rubbed the side of her neck, carefully avoiding a brush with her ear. A moment later the other hand passed across her
eyes; then, lightly, she touched it to her
cheek. But there were no tears, only the slick
coating of perspiration. No tears. Not anymore. They had brimmed and fled in hysterical spasms several months before, and what
remained had been sponged by the traces of
her nightmares.

Calm, she told herself. Stay calm. It's only
a dream, now.

One final massage, and she eased herself
carefully off the bed and draped a tattered
silken robe over her shoulders. Her feet slid
unerringly into thickly lined slippers, and
with one hand skimming along the wall, she
moved to the bedroom's threshold without
the necessity of a lamp. She leaned heavily
against the jamb; though she hadn't yet
glanced at her watch, she knew it was close
to dawn and there would be neither sense
nor progress gained from making another
attempt to sleep.

Resigned, then, she slid her arms into the
robe and waited until her eyes adjusted to
the dim light. The house was cored by a
central stairwell, and when she could make
out the cream-and-white bannister that
rimmed it, she stretched out a hand and
guided herself along the polished wood until
she reached the top step. Behind her, the

curtained french doors leading onto the back porch deck glowed faintly, and below, through the frosted panes of the front door, she could see the front light shimmering a winter white.

Now that's a bloody waste, she thought. Sam, of course, had insisted and she had fallen into the habit without really thinking; but perhaps, finally, it was time for a change.

She nodded, and while she descended, considered her present alternatives: if she turned left into the crowded living room, she might be tempted to lie down on the divan to watch the sun come up. No. She had had enough of the voices for one night, for one year. She thought it best not to press her sanity's luck.

The dining room directly opposite across the tiny slate-floored entrance hall would be just as useless for peace of mind, and probably just as dusty—the room had scarcely been used since Ben had died, and it was only procrastination that kept the double doors opened.

So, then. The kitchen it would be. As usual. As always.

And once decided, she grabbed the newel post, spun herself to the right and rushed down the green carpeted corridor toward the rear of the house. At the kitchen entrance she paused and snaked a hand around the jamb to flick on the ceiling light. A quick glance to the back porch, to the locked door of the den at the opposite end of the rear hall, and she escaped into fluorescent brightness. Immediately she busied herself with copper teapot and chrome toaster, plum jam and skimmed milk. A wall clock of Aztec design buzzed softly, the refrigerator switched on and comforted, and the blast of the kettle's steam shriek was less strident than welcome.

But when her fussing ended and she could find no other excuse to keep from sitting, she took her place at the circular table under the window and waited for daylight.

And here we are again, she thought, shaking her head at the tea that burned her tongue and the unavoidable sensation that this year's dream had been markedly less intense than any of the others. Had she taken Sam's advice and visited a psychiatrist, she probably would have been told by now that the grief-and-terror combination was finally being dulled by the clichéd sands of time that heals all wounds and colors psychic scars in autumnal shades. Well, maybe it was true. Maybe she was finally shedding her mourning skin. But the feeling left an indefinable emptiness all the same.

Yet it had been so exciting in the beginning. Her marriage to Ben Windsor had happened so swiftly, she still had to wonder how it had lasted as long as it had. She supposed it was a miracle. But what, then, would you call his murder?

With nothing and no one to tie her to the outside world, Natalie had arrived at Oxrun Station to assume a position at the local library. She had been twenty-five, fresh from her Master's and looking forward to the decent burial of several hapless affairs. There were plans to move on to larger communities after a year or so of paid apprenticeship, but Oxrun's gentle isolation, insulation and nearly tangible aura of unassuming wealth soothed her and her plans were buried along with her lovers. She had known it was more fitting to a schoolgirl, but she'd even entertained fantasies of a Nordic scion hoisting her bodily from behind the front desk and riding off to the hounds while she bore him the demigods who would continue his line. It was somewhat of a shock, then, when Ben had lumbered his six-and-a-half foot bulk up to a magazine display she was readying, introduced himself as the Assistant Chief of Police and, ten minutes later, invited her out to dinner. Flustered and oddly flattered, she'd stepped back, tipped over the rack and, in the confusion, accepted. And again, a week later. Then to a party. To a picnic. A long summer's drive through the woodlands of western Connecticut where they discovered a beaver's dam, a cave filled with bats, a rotted log swarming with honey bees; and where they had made not-so-gentle love on the banks of a pond rippling under the weight of several dozen geese.

Two months afterward they were engaged. Another seven months and the wedding in the stone church on Williamston Pike.

She hadn't minded his being a policeman

in Oxrun Station, even after she'd learned it
was his brother, Sam, who was the Assistant
Chief soon to be promoted. In the affluent,
unostentatious community crimes generally
ran to wavelets of petty vandalism and minor drug busts. Drifters were not tolerated,
and either soon found employment or a lift
to Mainland Road and a pointed finger toward
distant Hartford. It was safe. Almost boring,
despite Ben's assurances that he would be
moving up to something bigger in just a
few short years. And in the meantime, for
her own amusement more than anything,
she had purchased a radio with a police
band and listened to the patrols' transmis-
sions, giggling and applauding Ben's sometimes cryptic, often clumsily hidden messages
that threatened to grey what hair his brother
had left. And when Ben moved on their
marriage's first night shift, she lobbied for
and received approval and custody of the
library's night hours. Her major justification
to the Council had been the welfare and
continued patronage of the students attending the local community college. The Station's Council had thought her a daring and
charming innovator; her Director, Adriana
Hall, thought her impulsively faddish. Natalie thought she was just being damned clever
for, when the library closed, she'd hurry
home to turn on the radio and listen until
the dead hours just before dawn; if anything
happened after she'd gone to bed, Ben's

voice, no matter how soft or complacent, would waken her instantly.

But he had died less than a year after it had all begun. Had been murdered. Brutally. Found flung over the hood of his patrol car with his throat slashed and his face mutilated almost beyond recognition. His right ear had been severed and placed between his teeth. Died? Had been murdered. Mrs. Jamieson was fictitious. And the killer had never been found.

She refilled her cup and nibbled unconsciously at a cold piece of toast.

When the mourning period had ended, both Sam and his wife, Elaine, launched a campaign to ease her out of town and, failing that, urged her to at least find another home as far from Fox Road as she could get. Natalie was initially too shocked to respond, then too stubbornly annoyed to succumb to their clumsy blandishments.

"I'm a grown woman, Elaine," she'd told her sister-in-law during one prodding session on the front porch. "What good would it do me to run away? Listen, I'm not morbid, you know. I'm not about to turn the place into a memorial, if that's what you're afraid of."

"But Nattie," the pudgy woman had whined, "there are such awful memories here. Now, Sam thinks—"

"Well, good for dear old Sam. Now, what I think is that I am not leaving. No way. And I really wish you'd leave me alone!"

But she hadn't, and Natalie wasn't surprised, had only prayed that she would. And it pleased her to watch the barely suppressed expressions of impending apoplexy on her double-chinned face when she donated Ben's clothes to several charities, his few books to a hospital library. His meager collection of baseball and bowling trophies she gave to Sam. The only thing she kept when the purge had been completed was a shoebox of memories she hadn't looked at for several months.

And on this particular morning, after a nightmare now more horrible in its persistence than its content, she wasn't sure what it was she was waiting for. The killer's apprehension? The next man in her life? The end of those dreams that clawed into her sleep for several nights running on the anniversary of Ben's death?

What, she wondered, and instantly and relievedly decided it was—had to be—all of them.

"But you're not going to get any of them by moping around drinking lousy hot tea," she told herself, laughing, and fearing as always that her habits were beginning to decline into the stereotype mold of the long-suffering, pining woman, the old maid, the pitiful (but not pitiable) husk of what had once been a woman who had enjoyed control— of herself, her life and, as much as she was able, her destiny. Fate, she'd concluded, was the poorer word because it denoted a manipulation beyond her grasp. Destiny, however;

she liked its sound and thought of it as a horizon on an unfinished canvas, undefined and waiting for her to get there so she would know what it looked like.

Hurrying her plate and cup into the dishwasher, she darted upstairs to shower away the sticky residue of her dream. Then she chose a snug pair of slacks and summer-thin blouse and slipped into the light overcoat she'd bought downtown the year before. It was an extravagance, a calculated defiance to those who continued to look upon her with hypocritical sorrow. She knew she was known to many in the Station as the Policeman's Widow. It annoyed her, then amused her. And no Policeman's Widow, certainly not in Oxrun Station, wore a bright gold coat with a thickly rich fox collar; nor in Oxrun did she allow her soft sable hair to fight with the wind for the privilege of nestling on her shoulders. Not a Policeman's Widow.

She laughed as she locked the front door behind her.

She stood on the porch of the small, square dark blue house and squinted at the sun poking between the homes opposite. It was a cool brittle morning, and the few birds remaining in the slowly shedding trees rose to greet her raucously. She grinned, took a deep breath and moved to the sidewalk, deliberately avoiding a glance to the left. Once past the three Victorian boxes that hunkered between her home and the corner, she paused with one hand resting on the green metal pole of a Dead End sign. The newborn brightness was decidedly too invigorating to waste arriving early to work. It would be much better for her to walk a mile or so to drive the stiffness from her legs, the patina of the evening from her eyes. In which direction, then? Straight on across Williamston Pike to stay on Fox Road would bring her directly to the police station, and the chance of encountering Sam. Into the sun two blocks would confront her with the library.

No choice, she thought as though she'd had one from the start, and she put the sunrise to her back. She would take the three long blocks to Mainland Road and turn around. A fair plan, an easy plan, and one she followed several times a week over the past four months.

So who, she asked herself, are you kidding, lady?

The collar brushed at her neck, tickled and made her laugh aloud. She adjusted the broad strap of her pocketbook over her shoulder, thrust her hands into her pockets and walked with broad relaxing strides. The homes she passed sat well back from the Pike, protected by high-trimmed hedges and trees nearly as old as the country around them. She paused only once, to allow a battered sedan to back onto the street and join the light traffic headed almost exclusively toward the highway. There was a bus stop on the next corner complete with a freshly painted white bench, but she ignored the temptation to sit, reveling too much in the tightness at her cheeks and the pleasantly sharp sting of cold air in her lungs. She crossed, heard the cough of a starting motor and turned. There was a patrol car parked opposite her, ostensibly keeping an eye on the outbound traffic. She shook her head slowly and resumed her walk.

Sam, she thought, is carrying his big-brother routine too far.

She had, in fact, mentioned this uncontracted surveillance several times, but each meeting only resulted in his smothering her objections under his own grand illusions of police proficiency and familial obligation. She had never before had the nerve to tell him she was no longer his kin; and with Ben gone, no longer wanted to be. Finally, her persistence penetrated and he admitted his men had more important matters to attend to, and she was relieved. And the absence of the blue uniform shadows helped in cutting away one more strand of the now fragile rope that tied her to the past.

But it had begun again. Unasked, and unexpected, and she hated Sam Windsor for spoiling her beautiful new day.

"No!" she said aloud to the empty sidewalk. "No, he will not do it to me again." And she lifted her head, hunched her shoulders against a gust of October wind, and watched through the traffic as the church where she and Ben had been married drifted slowly by. It was a long and aging structure that had suffered with little dignity the ravages of recent parishioner neglect. Its once clean stone had become blemished with dark, unsavory blotches of some unknown fungus. Its steeple was silent even on Sundays because there was no money left to repair its pre-Revolutionary bell. The double front doors needed new paint, and the stained glass was dull even when lighted from within. Reverend Karl Hampton did much of the handyman work himself, and as a result the rectory beside it suffered as well. Not that he seemed to care overly much. The last time Natalie saw him, he'd been picking out a new Mercedes at a local dealer. His patrician priorities, she thought, obviously weren't monastic.

She frowned, ducked away as a truck blasted dust into her face, then hesitated as though she would cross to take a closer look. The frown deepened to a scowl, however, when the patrol car slid into view.

Confound it, I won't have this!

She quickened her step and nearly tripped over the broken curb at Devon Street. She grabbed onto a Stop sign to keep herself from tumbling into the gutter. Another gust, and fur from her collar slid into her mouth. She spat, brushed stiff fingers through her hair, and made a show of examining the houses until she reached Mainland Road.

Trucks, then, and crowded buses interlaced

with automobiles in a swift tide passing in both directions without turning into the Station. Commuters heading for the far larger towns north and south, never once seeing Oxrun to the east nor the checkered expanse of unused farmland to the west. Blind they seemed, and Natalie had long ago stopped thinking it sad that her town was continually ignored. Now she believed the community quite large enough. So let it stay a whistle-stop, she thought; it makes things a lot more simple that way.

She waited five minutes for a break in the traffic, then ran across the Pike and headed back into the sun. Almost immediately she reached one of the few businesses this side of Fox Road: the low profile, red-brick home of the *Station Herald.* Its plate-glass window was undecorated except for the gold Gothic lettering of the paper's name, and a taped front page of the previous week's edition. Peering inside, she could see the ceiling's embedded fluorescent lights already glowing, and a dim shadow figure obscured by the sun's glare raised a hand in greeting. She waved back, slowed, and when the office door opened, stopped in feigned surprise, smiling broadly and tugging self-consciously at the collar of her coat.

"Hey, there, lady," a man said gaily, "you always walk the streets in the middle of the night? You could get mugged or something, you know."

Natalie laughed at the warning she never

took seriously, nor ever tired of hearing. "In case you're interested, my fine-feathered reporter, it's going on nine o'clock."

"And that," the young man said, "is definitely the middle of the night. You thirsty?"

And before she could object, he reached out and put a hand to her elbow. "Come on in. It's cold outside, and I need a little bookish sympathy."

Natalie glanced at the patrol car now stationed less than fifty yards away, and nodded. Sam, she thought, I sure hope your boys are taking notes.

"Coffee? Oops, sorry, I forgot. You're one of those uppity folk who think coffee drinkers are on the road to perdition. Tea, lemon and sugar, right?"

She nodded and sat in a stiff-backed chrome chair by the first of a half-dozen desks arranged in a ragged file away from the window. Along the side wall, teletypes were already clattering to a shirt-sleeved man hunched in front of them, a pad and pencil in his liver-spotted hands. A young woman stood by a water cooler combing her hair. The rear wall had been divided in half: on the left the same walnut paneling that carried all the way to the front, and a door that led to the printing plant in back; on the right there was glass festooned with snippets of articles and headlines, and beyond it the boxlike office of Wagner Dederson, editor and publisher. By straining, Natalie could see past the maze of paper and recognized Dederson's overweight and overdressed figure apparently in argument with someone who, she thought with a start, was Karl Hampton.

"Hey."

She blinked and grinned sheepishly, and wondered how much of that brash newsman image Marc Clayton polished from his watching old movies, and how much was natural. It was, at times, a little too much to take, but she flattered herself in believing it was a role he practiced solely for her.

"So how've you been, Marc?"

He took his chair and placed it in front of her, sat and put two paper cups on the desk. He was no more than an inch taller than she, slight, pale, and constantly neglectful of the white blond hair that straggled over his ears and forehead. He wore gold wire-rimmed glasses with rectangular lenses and spent more time fighting their slide down the bridge of his uptipped nose than looking through them. At the moment, she thought critically, he looked as though he hadn't even been home to shave, and tried to picture him with a beard and moustache. It wouldn't suit him, she decided; he would look like a kid trying to be old.

"How have I been?" he repeated slowly, as if the question was philosophically impossible to answer in less than an hour. Then he shrugged and glanced away from her impatient stare. "Lousy, if you must know. I've nearly been canned again, and the landlady refuses to fix a roof that leaks right over my bed, and if I get one more story of mine slashed again, I'm going to pack up and head for fame and fortune in the big city." Then he laughed at the dismay in her face. "Well, you asked for it, you know."

"I think I'm sorry I did. The roof is nothing new, but what about the firing?" She nodded toward Dederson's office. "He getting testy in his old age?"

A wave of his hand almost tipped over the cups, neither of which they'd touched. "Dederson thinks I lean too much toward the purple-prose school of journalism."

"And what's that supposed to mean?"

"It means I imagine things that aren't there and then write about them as if they were the apocalypse. Like the creeps last week that smeared black paint all over the synagogue on Devon, down past Chancellor. I said they seemed to be taking part in a conspiracy to defame all the religious community's edifices in town. Dederson says it was a bunch of drunken college kids feeling their oats."

"Well, weren't they?"

"Who knows? They weren't caught. And neither were the poor, underprivileged kids who sliced up the altar cloth and dented the crucifix at St. Mary's last month. Or the rambunctious students who nailed those dead cats to the Baptist Church doors last June." He frowned, drained his cup without breathing and dropped it into a wastebasket. "A conspiracy? Nuts. Just kids feeling their enriched oats."

"It could be, you know," she said, at once taken by the seriousness of his tone, and the nervous way he pulled at the tie sloppily knotted and yanked toward the middle of his chest. "I mean, you read about it all the time, don't you? Rich kids with nothing better to do, so they—"

"I know, I know. That maybe I could believe. But . . ." He stopped, suddenly, and swiveled to his desk. "Nat," he said without looking at her, "how've you been lately? Seriously."

Puzzled, she could only lift a hand to indicate she was doing fine.

"You, uh, over the hump, so to speak?"

"Oh." And she surprised herself by saying. "Yes, I think so. Life, as they say, goes on whether you want it to or not." Her smile was a weak one. "So they say. Why?"

Marc rubbed at his chin before extracting a crumpled sheet of paper from an untidy pile on his blotter. "There was a murder last night, Nat. In the park. Howard Vorhees, the assistant dean of students out at the college."

"I don't think I want to hear anymore, Marc," she said. Then, sighing, nodded for him to continue while a tightness around her chest amplified the increased beating of her heart.

Vorhees, Marc explained, was found just after dawn stretched out on a bench near the ball field. His clothes had been stripped off and tossed into a nearby briar copse. A copy of the *Herald* had been placed carefully over his face. When the officer who'd discovered the body pulled back the paper, he found the throat slashed, the face mutilated apparently by a razor, and his right ear had been cut off and stuffed into his mouth. Chief Windsor had admitted to no leads and had doubled the park patrol immediately.

"As of," and Marc glanced at his watch, "as of twenty minutes ago, there were no clues of any kind. No tracks, no nothing." He flicked the paper with a forefinger and set it carefully back on the pile. "I also got into trouble because Dederson wanted me to interview you, and I told him where he could find it if he wanted it that bad."

Natalie swallowed the trace of bile that had crept into her mouth. A feeling of time displacement unsteadied her, and she felt the coffee cup pressed into her hands. She sipped gratefully, not tasting the cool liquid, and handed it back.

"It's the same, isn't it?"

He agreed, sadly. "And when I mentioned that instead of an interview we ought to pursue the possibility of a connection, he told me, and I quote for your edification, 'Clayton, if you want to be a mystery writer, then move to the city. You, sir, are a reporter. That means you report, get it? Report, Clayton, or cover your typewriter and truck.'"

"Truck?" She laughed once, loudly.

"Truck," Marc said. "He likes to think he's up on the latest street language."

She pulled her purse into her lap and toyed nervously with the strap. "What are you going to do?"

"If I knew, I'd tell you. Come on," he said, grabbing his brown and rumpled sports jacket from the back of his chair. "I'll walk you to work. That was where you were headed, wasn't it?"

"Where else? I still have bills, you know."

And once on the street, they separated just enough to keep their arms from brushing as they walked.

It was a confusing few minutes. Natalie wished Marc wouldn't be quite so sensitive about her feelings, her image, but she was also pleased at the consideration. Several of her friends had not so subtly wondered why she and Marc hadn't been seeing more of one another, and lately Natalie had discovered she was thinking along the exact same lines. Especially now.

"It was the same," she repeated as they crossed Fox Road and slowed to stretch the last two blocks before the library.

"It was, Nat. That's why I told you. I thought you had a right to know."

"I don't really," she said, "but thanks, anyway."

"I hope I haven't wrecked your day. I have a habit of doing things like that."

"You haven't," she said truthfully.

He nodded, greeted loudly a mailman leaving the corner post office, and took her arm again to take her across Centre Street. As she glanced down the only business street in Oxrun, Natalie closed her eyes briefly and squeezed his hand between her arm and side. Had Sam been the one to give her the news, it was possible she would have succumbed to the roiling her nerves were threatening, but Marc's firm grip and the comforting drone of his rambling voice had an effect she hadn't expected. It was odd, and she wondered if perhaps she wasn't reading too many of the library's romances lately.

"For crying out loud," he muttered suddenly and stared at the traffic. "There goes Dederson down to the police station. That means I'll have to watch the shop." He grinned. "Now I won't be able to paw you behind the stacks." He released her arm, leaned slightly toward her before nodding brusquely and whirling to run back toward his office.

Well, I'll be ... Natalie thought as she watched him. I think the dope was going to kiss me.

Chapter 2

THE LIBRARY still seemed spring-new after four New England years. A red-brick rectangle, it was fronted by two-story arcs of polarized glass weekly washed and giving it a distinctly churchlike appearance. Surrounding the building were three narrow concentric aprons of white concrete that served as footpaths between wire-braced saplings of birch and willow. Four large squares of lush grass still a summer green stretched from the steps to the sidewalk and were bordered by redwood benches, today occupied by several elderly men bundled in grey and brown and playing checkers. Natalie had never understood why they didn't prefer the municipal park that began only one block further on, but she liked to believe it was the stimulation of proximity to her books. Soon enough, however, the weather would add an uncomfortable dampness to its autumn bite and like aged birds too weary for migration, the men would retreat inside to one of the reading rooms off the main lobby where the warmth more often than not would put them quickly to sleep until closing.

She nodded to several of the regulars, and they smiled back at her absently, tolerantly. Then she turned her back to the morning wind and watched Marc hurrying out of sight. There was a momentary temptation to call out, to make him return, but sudden warning shouts of a trio of bike riders broke her resolve. Regretfully, she went inside.

With vaulted ceiling and yard-long cylinders of light suspended by gold-and-black chains, the main floor was cavernous and bright, though its patrons' voices automatically hushed upon entering as though in the presence of an ancient cathedral. Natalie scanned the area immediately before her as she slipped out of her coat, surprised that there were already a handful of people back in the stacks and several more scattered at the round tables that were oaken islands on the pale blue carpeting. To her left, the walls were colored with shelves of current fiction, to the right the yellow, red, green cheer of the fairy-tale mobiles suspended over the children's section. Directly ahead was a formidable horseshoe desk which she avoided carefully as she drifted toward the aluminum steps that led up to the gallery and the library's offices. A man whispered a hello and she whispered back, smiling. A boy not more than ten scurried around her with an armful of books, plopping them noisily on the counter of the desk and hopping impatiently as a middle-aged clerk took her time checking them out.

Natalie almost changed direction to goad some speed into the woman, but the frantic waving of a girl ten years her junior distracted her. She waited, then took the first steps up as the girl stepped into her shadow.

"I've put the mail on your desk, Mrs. Windsor," Miriam Burke said breathlessly, "and Chief Windsor has called twice already—boy, does he ever sound ticked off!—and did you hear about the guy that was killed in the park last night? Gory. I wish I could have seen him. He was from the college, you know, but I never met him. Mrs. Hall called, too, to remind you about Monday's staff meeting—do you know who's going to get the ax this time? And do you think it would be okay if I left early today? I know I promised to stay with you, but there's this guy I met who wants to take me to this really super party tonight and I have to—"

"Stop!"

Natalie leaned against the metal railing that curved with the steps toward the center of the gallery. She shifted her coat to her other arm and smiled down at the girl. Miriam's sweaters and summer blouses, and the long ebon hair parted in the center were instant and sometimes disconcerting refutations of the sexless librarian image prevalent

in most small towns; and though her New
York City accent grated at times, her infec-
tious ebullience was something neither Natalie nor the autocratic Mrs. Hall would have
traded for a dozen more efficient workers.
And Miriam was the closest thing to a friend
Natalie had at work.

"Miriam," she said lightly, "who in God's
name winds you up in the morning? Don't
you know it's Saturday and people—normal
people—are supposed to be asleep this hour
of the morning? And will you quit calling me
Mrs. Windsor! It makes me sound like an old
maid."

Miriam gaped, blinked slowly and pushed
a nervous hand through her hair. There was
a confusion of apology and disorientation in
her face, and Natalie, wanting to laugh, placed
a hand on her shoulder instead.

"Hey, relax, girl, will you? This isn't big
business, you know, or one of those gigantic
corporations that are practically fascist in
tolerating laxness. It's only a library, for
crying out loud. And sure you can leave
early. Don't worry about it."

"But what about Mrs. Hall?"

"It's Saturday, Miriam, remember? She'll
be hung over until Monday, at least."

Miriam tried a grin to show she understood, and Natalie turned her stare to the
main floor. At the desk, Arlene Bains was
flipping through the clumsily large pages of
the Fine Book, scowling but failing to cower
a tall boy in a football jersey standing decid-

edly unrepentant in front of her. Natalie shook her head. The tall, fog-haired woman was trying to emulate her husband, Simon, but her heart was never in it. If Miriam, Natalie thought, was the antithesis of the mythical spinster librarian, then Simon Bains was the archetypal miser who also happened to own a prosperous bank. Poor Arlene just wasn't measuring up.

"Look," she said to Miriam, "if you get too serious about all this, you're going to end up as sour as Arlene. God forbid."

And without waiting for a response, she hurried up to the gallery and into her office.

There were three offices off the gallery itself. The largest was Mrs. Hall's, strategically in the center. On the right was an office currently being used as a storeroom, and the smallest, on the left, was Natalie's by default.

It would have been little more than a fair-sized bedroom in an average house, and was now jammed with stacks of new unstamped books, magazines to be sampled for possible subscription, and several cartons recently arrived from a local church's supply drive. It was, she thought as she waded through to her desk, more a physical challenge than an administrative one, and she knew it was the butt of several longstanding jokes among the staff. Most of the teasing was pleasant, though there were spots of bitterness from those who had been passed over for promotion when Natalie rapidly proved herself the most competent. The rancor had concerned her at first, but since Ben's death, she had cared little for the dueling of provincial politicking and had always been nervously grateful when Adriana managed to replace her most persistent detractors with young trainees from the college.

She didn't know what she had done, though it had to have been inadvertent, to gain Mrs. Hall's support, and the thought made her even more determined to help the woman out of a depression that had dogged her since the spring. The way things stood now, however, the Director would have no sympathy or understanding that didn't come bottled in bond, warm, with a dash of soda.

"Well," she said to the posters on the wall, the windows back and side, "here we go again."

For several hours, then, she was busy with invoices, inventories, queries from patrons and employees. She took several minutes, but no more, to worry about the lack of a sufficient budget proposal for the approaching fiscal year. She skimmed magazines, ran downstairs in time to hear Miriam reading an *Oz* book to an entranced circle of children, returned in the wake of a snap from Arlene that she could use another assistant on the floor. There was thankfully no time to think, to consider what Marc had told her until well past noon when she asked Miriam to dash around the corner to the Centre Street Luncheonette and fetch her back a hamburger, salad and malted.

And while she waited, a call from the desk brought her down to the main floor. A middle-aged woman in a lamb's wool coat was standing impatiently in front of Arlene, whose eyes were rolled to the ceiling in search of guidance. Natalie smiled immediately, professionally, when the woman snapped her glare around.

"You're Mrs. Windsor?" The voice was nasal and reed brittle.

Natalie nodded.

"Well, I must say, you certainly don't run an efficient library around here."

"What's the trouble, Arlene?" she said, ignoring the woman as politely as possible.

"She wants something by Bishop Sheen. There are four books in the catalogue but ..." and she waved a hand to the card file. "None of them are out, and I keep trying to tell her they're missing, I guess, but—"

"But nothing," the woman said angrily. "I put in my reserve for that book over a month ago."

"But, madam," Natalie said, "if they're missing, there's nothing we can do but reorder them. Have you tried the county library?"

"All that far?" The woman was incredulous. "You must be joking. I haven't got that kind of time. I think I shall have to speak to Mrs. Hall about this." She headed for the stairs, stopped when she saw the closed door above her and made a smart about-face to the exit. Natalie watched her, shook her head sympathetically at Arlene and returned to

her office. Four books. By Bishop Fulton
Sheen. But she had no time to wonder when
Miriam returned with lunch.

"How do you do that?" Miriam asked as
she watched Natalie gulp at a malted.

Natalie raised her eyebrows.

"I mean, how can you eat that stuff all the
time and still stay so thin?"

Natalie grinned around her straw, peeked
at the slight curves under her blouse and at
her waist, then up to the more rounded
figure Miriam swore was 90 per cent fat. She
leered, Miriam laughed, and the room was
silent again.

A break, she told herself as she finished the
last of the burger, and stood quietly at the
side window looking out at the park across
the street. The trees were still bright in their
dying, the grass a deceptive green. Over the
piked top of the black iron fence she could
see riders through the shrubbery cantering
their horses along the bridle path, women
pushing baby carriages and gossiping as
though their children didn't exist. A lonely
kite of orange and white punched through
the foliage and strained to carry its rag tail
to the horizon. Moving to one side, she
pressed a cheek against the cool window and
saw a patrolman station himself opposite the
High Street entrance. He knelt to speak with
a little girl and her doll, waved a group of
teen-aged boys away from the flow of pedes-
trian traffic that Natalie thought would be
making detours to see the scene of the recent

crime. He stretched, then, and walked over to the curb where he accepted a cup of obviously hot liquid from the driver of a patrol car that idled at the crosswalk.

When the telephone interrupted her, she jumped and thought of Sam.

Swore silently when she recognized his voice.

"Nattie, why the hell haven't you called me? It's been over a week."

She grinned maliciously at a poster of Big Ben on the unpainted wall. "I've been busy today, Sam. I'm sorry, really I am."

"All right." The voice was deep, well-suited to the man's size. "I, uh, just wanted to tell you, see, that we—"

"Don't bother, Sam. I've already spoken with Marc Clayton down at the *Herald*. He read me the fact sheet you put out. Is that why you've got me tailed again?"

"Tailed?"

She was annoyed, and suddenly impatient. "Come on, Sam, I'm too busy and too tired to play your manly games. You've got a patrol on me again, and I don't like it. It's invasion of privacy, or something like that."

"Nattie, it's protection and you know it."

"Protection?" She coughed loudly to keep her voice from breaking too high. "Protection from what? I'm not the one who's dead, Sam." And immediately she said it, she bit her lower lip. "Sam? I'm sorry. I didn't mean it that way. It was uncalled for."

"It's okay," but it didn't sound that way to her. "I just don't want you hurt, that's all."

"Sam, I appreciate the thought, really I do. But I'm not about to have another go around with you. Ben's been dead over a year and a half, and there's nothing to connect me with that poor man's murder this morning. I don't know him. I never met him in my life. There is no reason at all that I can see for this new so-called protection."

"Hey, what do you mean, so-called?"

"Just what I said, Sam. It isn't protection until I need it, and I've just said I don't. I'm old enough to take care of myself. And," she said louder, sensing he was about to interrupt, "it's ruining my social life."

"What social life?"

She bridled at the sneer behind the words and began wrapping the phone cord around her wrist. "That's exactly what I mean, Sam. I haven't got one because who wants to go out with a woman whose shadow wears a badge?"

There was a silence through which she could hear the squad room's phones, a woman's voice pitched in righteous anger. Out of his private office and down with the boys, she thought. There was ribald laughter, and the woman began shouting.

"All right, Nat," he finally said. "You've made your point. I'll pull it off right away."

"Great," she said. "And if I get killed, it'll be my own fault and I'll apologize."

"That wasn't funny, Nat. Ben was my brother."

"No kidding, Sam. You could have fooled me."

Quickly she yanked the receiver away from her ear before the sharp crack of disconnection could deafen her. Then she sat and wondered what had gotten into her. She certainly could have been more reasonable, less argumentative. But in speaking without preparation or thinking, she knew she had told Windsor what she'd been wanting to say for months and had never had the courage.

Well, she told herself, it's done and there's no sense worrying about it, right?

There was no answer. Miriam barged in, and the last rush began before the staff vanished on its weekend break.

At five o'clock, an hour before leaving, she finally left her office and moved the paperwork remaining to the main desk. She disliked sitting alone when the others had left, more so now because of the images skirting her mind like cellar noises in a house after midnight. There were three lights burning at the back of the stacks, and one of the cylinders still glowed overhead. Outside she could see the street lamps hazed by the polarized glass, and the traffic's headlights were disembodied and brief.

The doors were locked. It was silent. With the thermostat dialed down, it was just this side of chilly.

When she sat, the level of the counter was even with her shoulders, and she didn't like the sensation of crawling out of a hole. It was then that she wished she had listened to Miriam, who had offered just before leaving to stay with her. Knowing the party was obviously something special, Natalie had demurred; she had also, she admitted, not wanted to have the girl prattle the sun down. For some reason she had decided her nearly three decades had not yet excluded her from the race of the young, and her efforts to play confidante were just as often comical as they were touching.

In addition, there was the project, her own private delving into an anomaly she still wasn't sure merited her time. From the locked drawer under a fold-down desk top, she pulled a series of distribution records, print-outs she'd ordered from the college computer hookup. Their length and bulk were too awkward to handle sitting down, so she reluctantly pushed back her chair and spread them out over the counter. It took several moments before her eyes adjusted to the simple computer coding, then she traced with her finger the usage frequency of each title in their inventory, marking several in red, underlining a score of others. Thirty minutes later the initial check was completed, and she took two steps back as though distance would sharpen her perception.

"A pattern," she muttered. "There must be some sort of pattern."

But the printout was too long, her nota-
tions too scattered, and she resigned herself,
sighing, to an evening of typing. On the other
hand, she thought as she pulled the typewriter drawer out and reset her chair, this
could be a damned fool's errand and I could
better spend my time elsewhere.

And where would that be? she wondered.
At home, as usual, curled up on the sofa
watching late movies, skimming the latest
fiction, forcing her way through the newest
reportorial exposés on government corruption.
There were times, of course, when an intrigu-
ing promotional blitz for a new film lured
her into the theater, but she seldom stayed
for more than an hour, and only once during
the past year had she seen a feature through
to completion. There was a restlessness that
gripped her in the flickering darkness, and
the artificial lives being dissected on the
screen seemed all too futile to bear watching.
Comedies were worse than drama; the picture she'd watched to the end had been a
French import without subtitles. She had
stayed only to test her ability to guess the
plot through gesture rather than words. When
it had finished, she didn't know whether she
had won or lost.

"Oh, shut up, Natalie!" she said, and leaned
back in the chair.

She could always call Marc and take him
up on any one of the several dozen rainchecks
she'd taken. Or even Karl Hampton, whose
monthly telephone calls exhorted her con-

stantly to whatever it was he called the finer
things in life. Perhaps Wayne Gernard, a
man who made her skin tighten whenever
she saw him. Reporter, minister, professor.
The cream of the crop, she thought, only the
best of Oxrun society for little old me
from. . .

Suddenly she yanked her purse from the
counter and rummaged until she located an
oval compact. Flipping its mirror up, she
stared at the image in the dim white light.
Thirty looking twenty, the schoolgirl profile
so many matrons coveted. A nose too stubbed,
ears too protruding to be truly attractive.
At times she wished she were a man so
she could grow a beard to hide the tiny chin
lost beneath full dark lips and high cheeks.
At times.

"And who will you be, my pretty little
maid," she whispered, "who will you be at
fifty?"

Ben was dead. Vorhees was dead. The
same murderer, or someone who had read of
the former and decided to imitate?

In the beginning, there had been an
uncharacteristic lust for revenge. A life cut
short—not Ben's, but hers. The drive faded,
however, dulled, because an intellectual game,
which had forced her to wonder about the
state of her emotions, had nearly stampeded
her onto the couch of the doctor Sam and
Elaine were urging upon her. But the game,
too, had lost its appeal, and until this morn-

ing, Ben's killer had gone the way of old Judge Crater.

It wasn't bravery, then, that had kept her in Oxrun, nor that brief tenure of vengeance.

With no family, few friends, there was no place else to go.

And the only reason she'd retained her married name was a need for an anchor outside her books.

"Enough," she said loudly, jumping at the faint echoes hovering in the high ceiling. She shook her shoulders and pulled the computer list to her. After a second's organization, she began to record the titles she'd marked. There was no carbon; she'd read once that carbons could be deciphered with the proper equipment, and unless she had actually discovered the makings of a conspiracy, she wanted no one to know of her clandestine scheme.

In the middle of the second page, the telephone rang.

"Hey, lady, are you still working?"

Still lost in the traces of what she was doing, Natalie didn't recognize the voice immediately; then, with a wrench, she shoved back from the typewriter.

"Marc, are you still working?"

"No fair answering a question with a question. Do you have any idea what time it is?"

She checked her watch and stifled a gasp when she saw the time was well past eight. "I had a lot to do," she said meekly.

"Yeah, right. Well, look, it's bloody cold out here. Do you mind if I come in and keep you company until you're done?"

Out here? She looked up and saw a faint shadow within the phone booth at the juncture of sidewalk and library lawn. She laughed, then, waved and hung up. A perfunctory check of her hair guided her to the door which she unlocked only when Marc came close enough to identify.

"You know," he said, hugging himself as he wandered back toward the counter, "I never did see what anyone would want with a mausoleum like this." He stared up at the darkness above the light, glanced at the shadows of books and magazines on the racks to the right of the desk. "I mean, libraries are no fun anymore. No dust, no snoring old men at the newspaper table, things like that." When he reached the counter, he picked up a portion of the printout and waved it. "See what I mean? Computers and everything. Whatever happened to that rotten old lady who wouldn't let me read anything in the adult section because it would warp my impressionable little mind?"

"You're looking at her," Natalie said mock sternly. "Only, I don't particularly think of myself as rotten."

"Just an expression," he said, and for the first time read the paper he was holding. "What's this? A list of books to burn?"

Gently she took the sheet from his hand.

"No, just taking inventory. Books get lost, you know. Happens all the time."

"Stolen, you mean."

She turned away and walked into the center of the horseshoe, hoping her movements seemed casual as she dropped the typewriter's plastic cover into place. "Yes, stolen, too. There are always people too cheap to buy books, and too lazy to bring them back."

"Ah, the scofflaw syndrome. I know it well."

"Don't tell me, sir, that the fine citizens of this community steal your newspaper?"

"Who? Us? Never. They don't dare, or we'll raise the price to a quarter instead of the long-dead dime. No, I mean the out-of-towners, such as they are, who use the parking meters and never pay up. Things like that."

This is ridiculous, Natalie thought, the dumbest conversation I've ever had. There was an impulse, then, to confide in Marc about her possible discovery, but it died unvoiced as he reached over the counter and snatched her coat from the back of the chair.

"Listen, lady," he said, "I have to be at a certain house tonight to cover a certain very important social event of the time. I had hoped to catch you earlier in order to ask—no, pray—that you come with me and keep me from dying of boredom."

"Then why go if you're going to be bored?" She joined him by the magazine rack and slipped into the coat before she knew what she was doing. "Why not just go home?"

"Because," Marc intoned, "Dederson commands. It's his way of getting back at me for the lousy articles he thinks I'm writing."

With a *moue* of sympathy and a pat on his shoulder, she gathered her papers together quickly and replaced them in the drawer, locked it and dropped the keys into her purse.

"It sounds to me," she said as she pushed him toward the door, "like I'm rather an afterthought in all this."

"Oh, now wait a minute, Nat—

"Hey," she said, using the master switch to turn off all the lights before pushing him outside, "calm down. I was only kidding."

He faced her, then, and cupped a hand to her elbow. "Nat, believe me, if nothing else in this world, you are definitely not an afterthought. Not with me. Not with anybody, for that matter. I didn't ask you before because I wasn't sure how you were going to take Vorhees' death, that's all."

Odd, she thought as they walked slowly to the sidewalk, but if that had been Sam talking, I would have been offended.

"What do you say?" he asked quietly.

The living room. The television. Hot cocoa and the wind blowing in from . . .

"I'll consider it very carefully."

They walked, and she was pleasantly conscious that he'd not released her arm, had in fact taken her hand by the time they'd reached her porch. It was a movement so natural there was no objection, and he said nothing until he peered through the darkness across her side yard. "How," he asked, "do you live with that thing out there?"

At the end of the street was a low cyclone fence topped with a double strand of barbed wire. During the growing seasons it was camouflaged by untended shrubbery and several massive willows; during fall and winter it was slightly imposing—less for its size than the clearly visible expanse of carefully mown grassland that stretched for over a hundred yards toward the newest section of the Oxrun Memorial Park. Sans moonlight, the tombstones and scatterings of ornate mausoleums were invisible, and with the sun the closest seemed only to be nothing more than sculptured boulders.

But Natalie knew what he meant. Simply the thought of settling near the neighboring dead had kept most of the homes bordering the cemetery empty for months at a time On her own street, hers was the only house occupied.

The graveyard's proximity had never bothered her, however. The visitors and mourners generally confined their activities to weekends and holidays, a time when she made it a silent point to keep the side windows curtained. The one or two stragglers who wandered over the grassy area were usually lovers looking for a place to test their courage.

She herself had gone to Ben's grave only twice; once for the funeral, and once a month later when she stood staring down at the words too neatly engraved in marble, waiting for a prayer, feeling only that she hadn't known her husband long enough to miss him more than she would a close friend.

"Actually," she said as she fumbled with the lock, "I kind of like it, you know? Shall I run through the gags about the peace and quiet and the neighbors and all that?"

"Not if you're going to be a deadly bore about it."

She groaned dutifully, pushed him into the living room and switched on all the Tiffany-style lamps. He flopped immediately onto the sofa and pulled open his coat. He was already dressed in dark suit and waistcoat, and a fleeting annoyance stiffened her until she remembered he would be attending the affair whether she accompanied him or not.

"You ever look at the older ones? The stones, I mean, from the Civil War, and like that?"

She nodded as she hooked her coat on the hall rack and took a quick look in its center mirror. "Once in a while, when I get to feeling too pompously immortal." She stood in the doorway, her hands clasped at her waist until, seeing herself posing, shifting them behind her. "Could you use a little coffee, Marc?"

"Nat, will you relax, for God's sake? I'm

not going to rape you, you know," He sat up
and rested his palms on his knees. "Come on,
Nat, go with me. It might not be as dull as
you think."

"I'll get your coffee," she said, and walked
stiffly past the stairs, habit stopping her long
enough to test the cellar door and again, the
knob to the den. Satisfied, and feeling oddly
foolish, she crossed back to the kitchen and,
with one hand on the stove, stared at her
reflection in the dark window glass. They
were fencing, maneuvering like characters in
a play speaking lines that had too much
meaning if they should only stop to listen.
She settled a finger lightly against her breast,
then pressed to see if she could feel her heart
pounding. Nothing, and she laughed at herself, stroked at her hair for comfort and
turned the burner on under the kettle.

"Hey, Nat!"

His voice startled her, not because she
didn't recognize it, but because it was something the house wasn't used to. She stepped
into the corridor and saw him standing by
the den.

"What's in here, Nat? Or am I being too
nosy?"

She was about to identify the room brusquely when something pushed her to his side.
"It's a den. Library. I don't know what you
would call it." She reached up over the door,
felt along the lintel and pulled down a
tarnished bronze key. She watched her hands
as they guided the key into the lock: They

weren't trembling, nor did they falter. And relief was like a spring breeze sweeping through a dusty room.

"Hey, Nat," he said while she fumbled for the light switch. "Hey, I didn't mean I wanted to poke my nose in here. I was just curious."

She looked at him and thought: *So am I.*

It was no bigger than the bedroom up-stairs, furnished simply with a pseudo-leather love seat, a walnut ash tray on a chrome stand perched next to a thickly upholstered arm chair. One bookcase built into the right-hand wall was empty. Under the window that looked out onto the yard was a second-hand secretary, and on it a shoe box bound with yellowed cord.

"I haven't been in here in months," she said, trying not to sneeze in the musty air. "When I clean, I plan to do a once over lightly." She shrugged. "Somehow I never get around to it."

"Ben's?" He was subdued, but there was an edge to his question that made her frown.

"Yes," she said, running a thumb over the box. "Before he'd go on duty, he would come in here to relax. Read a little law, or a mystery, or some notes on the two or three big cases he'd have once a year."

"You weren't allowed?"

She thought while she opened the box and dipped her fingers inside. "It wasn't so much that I wasn't allowed. I just didn't feel right, I guess." She grinned and held up a gold ring. "His one big gift to himself. He said he'd seen it in a film and had ordered one made like it, hoping it would add something to his image." She laughed, shook her head, and dropped the ring back.

"Well, let me tell you something, lady. I'd never—" Marc stopped and stepped back into the corridor. "Hey, your kettle's screaming."

Natalie tried to hurry the cord back into place, failed and left it. When she closed the door behind her, Marc handed her the key and stared at it so obviously that she had to smile as she put it back on the ledge again without using it. Then she brushed past him and worried at the stove until the coffee had been poured.

"Say," he said quietly as he took a chair at the table. "I just had this feeling that I'm imposing. I mean, here I am trying to sweep you out of the house, and all I'm really doing is prowling and making you play hostess and . . ." He sputtered and looked so discomfited that she wanted to lay a maternally soothing hand on his head.

"Don't worry about it." She placed cup and saucer in front of him and smiled. "If I'm acting a little strange, it's because I'm not used to . . . well, it's been a while, you know, since I've had visitors . . . like you."

He relaxed, then, and blew gently at the steam rising into his face. "Natalie, sometimes I worry about you. Really I do. This isn't exactly the most compromising position in the world, you know."

"Cut it right there!" she snapped. "We'll have none of that! None."

He seemed surprised at her vehemence, and somewhat stricken. But she couldn't resist the stirrings of faint panic, couldn't stifle the notion that unless she stayed on her guard, Marc would walk boldly in where she hadn't allowed a man for too long a time. Despite the scoffing that instantly replaced the fear, she kept telling herself it was too soon, that she needed more time.

And that, she knew, was just as much a deception as the idea that Oxrun Station was a perfectly normal town.

"I'll go," she said finally, pricking the weighted balloon that had been pressing on her lungs. "But only on one condition."

"Name it."

"That if he's there, you have to keep me away from Wayne Gernard."

Marc blinked in surprise. "You mean the college professor? He of the fat hands and portly cummerbund? That Wayne Gernard? You mean that oily slime pit has his sights set on you?"

"You know something," she said, leaning forward on her palms in front of him. "I'm not surprised you never got married, Marcus Clayton. Your knowledge and respect of and for the sensitivity of a woman's vanity is quite a bit less than zero."

He bowed mockingly and pointed at her

clothes with his cup. "May I suggest, however, that the sensitivity of the crowd we are about to suffer would be less challenged if you were to change into something less, shall we say, provocative?"

Instinctively, she looked down at the filmy blouse and ran her hands sensuously over her hips. "If I went topless, do you think anyone would notice?"

"Do you want another sample of my sensitivity, or a truthful answer?"

"Drop dead, Clayton, and drink your foul coffee. The dishwasher's over there. Clean up when you're done. I'll be down in a minute."

Chapter 3

"THEY SHOULD be marble," Marc said. He stood in the center of the small foyer and pointed to the stairs as she descended. Then he held out his hand and waited, patiently.

Her gown was a brown-and-gold caftan girdled at the waist by a wide white band. A matching tassel dangled from her right hip, and a cowl trimmed in crimson was folded against her back. It was an impulse, choosing this outfit, and she only knew that it tended in some unfathomable way to guide men's appreciative glances first to her feet sandaled in brown, then swiftly to her eyes that were a green so deep they were often mistaken for black. The looseness of the woolen cloth pleased her for the illusion of buxomness it created, and the flow it lent to her short-paced walk. It wasn't what she would have ordinarily worn on such an occasion, but Marc's cynicism had rubbed off, and it felt delightfully fresh. The Widow, she had decided in front of the bathroom mirror, would strike again.

Without a word he draped her coat over her shoulders, buttoned his own to the throat and escorted her outside. Darkness, save for the single dim street light, was nearly absolute; a rustling of the willows signaled a breeze in from the cemetery.

"We could walk to my place to get my car," he said, obviously not relishing the idea, and she dipped into her evening purse and pulled out a single silvered key.

"The garage, Marcus. My carriage."

He jumped the four steps to the walk and ran across the lawn to the garage. A moment later his curses made her laugh. The hinges of the double doors were rusted stiff and did not give easily to those in a hurry. Then she shook her head as he backed the grumbling Oldsmobile into the street and slid out to lean disgustedly against the roof.

"Tell me, librarian, how old is this thing?"

"Not quite as old as I am," she said, flashing him a smile before taking a seat.

"I wouldn't bet on it. It must have more holes on the bottom than the Swiss have cheese."

"Not very original," she commented wryly.

"Crap. The thing's falling apart."

"You would rather walk?"

He groaned, switched on the headlights and pulled away from the curb.

Onto the Pike and left, they remained

silent as they passed the dark library and
followed the park's northern boundary. The
iron fence was nearly invisible under trees
that dipped wearily down to the sidewalk,
gleaming only when a street lamp shattered
its light through the leaves that remained.
There were no pedestrians. And it was an
uncomfortable effort to keep from staring
through the darkness and imagining the scene
of the assistant dean's murder. Then she
heard it again: Ben's final puzzling transmis-
sion, the scream, and the sound of a heavy
weight falling before the radio crackled with
orders from Control to the other patrols.

It shouldn't be happening again, she thought
nervously. Nothing like that should happen
twice in anyone's life.

"I'm not a rich man, but I'll give you a
penny, Nat."

His voice was quiet, lulling in the green
glow of the dashboard. She shifted closer to
escape the chill that crept in through her
window, stopping only when her leg touched
his. She hated October. Its brilliant foliage
was only a cover for the dirges of December,
and the sharp advent of frost in the morning
only reminded her of January days when
getting warm had lost the gamelike quality of
earlier years.

"Nothing," she said when he repeated the
offer for her thoughts. "What is this celebration you're dragging me to?"

"Some celebration," he said. "Mr. Ambrose
Toal has decided to erect a new statue in the

park. At the instigation, it is said, of his dear
wife, Christine. It is to be a memorial, mind
you, to those in Oxrun Station who gave up
their lives in the service of their country. It
is also, and not so cleverly so, a husband-
hunting expedition for his equally dear daughter and woman of the world, Cynthia. Better
known to those who can pick out her window as Cynthia the—"

"Hold it!" she said. "I don't think I want
to know."

"What are you, jealous? Or just a prude?"

Her laugh was more like a bark. "I take it
you're supposed to write up this affair as the
highlight of the season, with ample descrip-
tions of m'ladies gowns, etcetera."

"Every disgusting pink cleavage."

Again they fell silent, and Natalie watched
the headlights tracing swaths of misted grey
along the tarmac. The park and clusters of
regular homes were gone, and in their place
the minor estates of the minor rich, feeble
and sometimes grotesque attempts at baro-
nial splendor complete with high walls, elec-
trified gates and aging uniformed guards.
Many of the homes had vanished over the
past decade, Marc commented without apparent sympathy, victims not only of rising
taxes and inflation, but also of Toal's insa-
tiable greed for space between himself and his
neighbors. Natalie said the area seemed as
much a graveyard as the one she could see
from her house.

"So, now we must needs wax philosophical?"

Marc said as he turned off the Pike onto a winding private road.

"Why not? Is there something better to talk about?"

And she clamped down on her tongue when she saw a frown crease his forehead and the hands stiffen on the steering wheel. Open mouth, insert foot, she thought as he parked the Olds behind a glittering line of foreign chrome. One of these days he's going to give you up as hopeless, woman, and then you bloody well won't have anything to worry about.

Toal's mansion was a bastardization of simple Georgian elegance and antebellum baroque. As they walked to the broad front steps, she winced at the immense veranda that apparently circumscribed the house and reduced to comic inanity the brick and stone stories that rose above it. It was as if Toal had seen one too many plantations on a flying tour of the Deep South and had decided his place could stand a little mint julep class.

A liveried Pakistani stood immediately inside the open front door, took their coats and directed them to a room on the left.

"Too much," Marc said as he fussed with his jacket.

Natalie said nothing.

The entrance hall was ballroom wide, floored in green marble and paneled in mahogany. A single constellation chandelier cast

multiple shadows and directed the eye down
to a staircase carpeted with intricate Persian
weave. Gilded Grecian benches were scattered along the walls, and the spaces between were occupied by the most dreadful
plaster copies of the French kings Natalie
had ever seen.

The front room was already crowded, doubled in size by mirrored walls, the ceiling
lowered by a drifting canopy of stale smoke.
Marc took her hand possessively and, after a
brief unconscious struggle, she submitted
long enough to be guided through the constantly shifting islands of lace and emeralds
and high-pitched conversation to a buffet
where bored-looking maids ladled a strong
tangy punch into deep crystal cups.

Natalie emptied hers at a gulp, held out
her hand unflinchingly for a refill. Marc
stared, grinned, and did the same.

"Now what?" she asked, unafraid of being
overheard. No one had paid them the slightest attention, and from an adjoining room a
band heavy on drums and bass guitar stifled
whatever impulses to eavesdropping there
might have been.

"Now we observe and learn, and wait for
Toal to make his appearance. He'll probably
give a little speech, show us a copy of the
statue; make another little speech and intro-
duce his family. Then we'll all go home
drunk in the knowledge that we have basked
in the unrelenting sun of the powerful arm of
capitalism."

"Hey," she said, "don't you think that's laying it on a little thick, even for you?"

He grinned an immediate apology and bowed at the waist. "Your point, lady. I'm sorry. It's just that I had other plans for this evening, and this definitely was not among them."

What questions she might have had, however, were forestalled by a hand that grabbed her shoulder and turned her around.

"Oh, Wayne," she said behind a forced smile. "I didn't think you went in for these things."

Professor Wayne Gernard preened his thick black moustache, reached out a thrice-ringed hand to take hers, lift it to his lips and kiss the air wetly above it. "Natalie, how wonderful. And I'm as surprised to see you as you are to see me. What brings you here?"

"Me," Marc said, leaning over her shoulder. "How are you, Wayne?"

"All things considered, not bad actually. My dear dean insists I attend Toal's foul wakes so he won't forget some century-old promise about a library for the new law school. I could have gone to a show in New Haven, you know."

"Sorry about that," Marc said unconvincingly. "We all have our crosses, don't we?"

It took a moment before Natalie was able to free her hand from Gernard's perspiring grip, and she stepped immediately back to allow the two men plenty of sparring room. Her back bumped against the buffet and she turned, nodded to a maid and accepted another cup.

This, she thought, is unreal. I'm not really here, you know. It's a television show about the four hundred, and I'm sitting on the living room floor in my flannel pajamas drinking diet soda and making rude comments. She sipped at the punch, then put a hand to her temple to still a quick wave of dizziness.

Marc, she saw, was grinning open-mouthed though the noise level had risen and prevented her from hearing what he was saying. Wayne was obviously uncomfortable, unaccountably nervous as he continually wiped a forefinger over his moustache, then tugged at the ill-fitting vest that kept bunching up toward his neck. She knew he was trying to carve Marc's profession with witticisms and barbs, but Marc was enjoying the bout; he had taken off his glasses and the resulting squint gave him an unsettling Fu Manchu remoteness. For me, she wondered, and was slightly incomprehensibly resentful. But it must be the drinks, she thought, because it wasn't often that she was able to play M'Lady to a joust.

There was a barking laugh from Marc, and the professor tried silencing him with an academic sneer. The guests beyond them had begun to shift as others arrived, however, and Natalie's attention was directed through an opening across the room to the front by the windows. Miriam was there, laughing and lifting a sparkling cup to the lips of a man a full head taller than she; he was, Natalie noted sardonically, apparently less interested in the refreshment than the buxom plunge of the diaphanous cocktail gown floating redly in front of him. A maximum of temptation, a minimum of cover—Adriana would have a fit if she could see that, she thought with a grin and suddenly hoped Miriam wouldn't try a little deep, heavy breathing. She stared pointedly for several minutes, hoping the young girl's eye would stray her way so she would have an opportunity to compare notes, and stand a little in the shadow of sanity.

But the opening closed before contact could be made, and before she could redirect Marc's attention away from Gernard, there was a flurry of motion at the far end of the room. The lights in their sconces dimmed and, as Marc had predicted, Ambrose Toal climbed to a makeshift stage, made a short inaudible speech, and pulled a cord which released a velvet curtain closed behind him. There, under a single lavender spotlight, was a four-by-five photograph of a statue: a nurse standing valiantly over the huddled and agonized bodies of wounded men in indeterminate uniform. Her hands were clasped to her pointed bosom, her blind eyes lifted piously toward an invisible sun. The face was undoubtedly Christine's—aquiline, soft, a careful aging around the mouth and eyes. Handsome was the word Natalie thought of at once, and it squared with the few glimpses she had had of the millionaire's wife—handsome and arctic cold.

A clumsy fanfare from the band and an enthusiastic explosion of applause and comment greeted the unveiling. Marc looked over his shoulder and rolled his eyes heavenward. Gernard stood at attention. There was a glare of flashbulbs, and Marc yanked a pad from his jacket pocket. *To work,* he mouthed with an exaggerated sigh. *Hurry back,* she whispered silently, shaking her head when his expression launched an invitation to go with him. He nodded, ignored Gernard and pushed his way up through the crowd. Natalie, too, decided to leave, not wanting to be alone with the professor, seeing already the words forming in his throat, questions about Vorhees and the connections with Ben. With a meaningless murmur she knew was falsely coy, she excused herself hurriedly and made her way back to the hall where the Pakistani coldly directed her to the powder room on the second floor. Thanking him, she set her empty cup on a chair more openwork than substance and took the stairs as fast as she could. There was a turmoil in her stomach that reminded her uncomfortably that she hadn't eaten anything since lunch; and the potent liquid from the punch bowl was not doing much to steady her equilibrium.

The anteroom was easily large enough, she decided, to contain both bedrooms in her own home. A maid dressed in starched white waited primly in a stiff-backed chair by the entrance and handed her a small towel, a mint scented bar of soap, and a small packet of flowered tissues. Natalie accepted the hand-outs gracelessly and sat on an upholstered bench on the far side of the room, her hands folded in her lap. Despite the bright lights reflected in the half-dozen woman-tall mirrors along the walls, she felt instantly cooler, and was startled then to feel perspiration gathering on her forehead. Carefully, she extracted a single tissue—smiling apologetically at the maid for the noise—and dabbed at her face. Then she rolled the moist tissue into a ball and, failing to locate a wastebasket, stuffed it into her full sleeve.

And now what? It was fine for Marc to be at the party; at least he had something to do to stave off boredom. But she knew few of the guests well enough to talk with, and those she had recognized she found herself avoiding because of the killing. There might be a chance to talk with Miriam later, but somehow she felt an intrusion would be definitely unwelcome at this stage of the young girl's not-so-subtle campaign.

So, then. She could mentally run through her list of books to find the pattern she was groping for; but when the first title grew hazy under the influence of the punch, she abandoned the idea and began to whistle silently. A minute later she looked up and saw the maid staring at her, not unfriendly but curious, and she rose at once and hurried into one of the several private cubicles set along the near wall in the adjoining, smaller room. Each held a petite vanity, oval mirror edged in silver, and settings containing make-up, combs, brushes and other bits of repair paraphernalia. Placing her purse on the ruffle-edged table, Natalie stared at her reflection and considered spending the next hour or two making faces at herself.

Then she made a perfunctory swipe at her hair, touched her little finger to the corners of her mouth, and pushed against the table in order to rise from the thick-cushioned stool when she heard two women move into the cubicle next to hers. They were arguing, and she decided this would be far better than being cornered by Gernard again. Who knows, she thought, maybe the gossip will be something Marc can use.

"A nightgown," one woman said, her voice trembling with indignation. "She was wearing a nightgown. I swear it!"

"Calm down, will you?" The second one was markedly younger, and more harsh. The words were slightly slurred. "I hardly think it will cause a scandal, you know. You're being ridiculous."

"I'm always ridiculous as far as you're concerned."

The sound of glass slapped onto the vanity, a stool shifted abruptly and slamming against the partition.

"Well, now you've torn it. Are we going to

spend the rest of the night sniping at each other, or are we going to get on with it?"

"Well, we can't very well do anything with her in the house, can we?"

"Mother, you're being simple again. What does she have to do with anything at this point? You're certainly not going to send her an invitation, are you?"

Natalie rubbed the side of her face slowly, turning around as cautiously as she could. If the so-called nightgown they had mentioned was, in fact, her own caftan, then it was she they were arguing over. A sudden wash of guilt made her decide to look for a way out without being discovered.

"I'm not sure I like it."

"You don't have to like it. Just do it, or he'll get mad."

"Well . . ."

"It's almost over, Mother."

"I suppose so. But what about her?"

Natalie tried angling a look at the mirror opposite the cubicle, but she knew she was eavesdropping on Christine and Cynthia Toal. But what was it they didn't like? And why couldn't she be around when whatever was going to happen happened? A piercing stab of ice along her spine made her stand, sway, reach out to brace herself against the partition. That it might entail some manner of crime momentarily frightened her, but a quick and vicious pinch at her hip caught the soaring panic, calmed it and forced her to think more sensibly.

"This is all very awkward, you know, my dear. I'm not sure Ambrose will like it one bit."

"For God's sake, will you stop worrying? As soon as he's finished with that shrimp, they'll be on their way. God Almighty, you'd think we were planning to rob a bank."

"Well, in a way we are, aren't we?"

"Oh, Mother, shut up!"

Natalie decided a swift retreat was the best defense against entrapment. She waited until the voices faded into whispers, then darted out of the cubicle, through the connecting door and into the corridor. She hoped their concentration on the mirror prevented them from catching a glimpse of her as she'd hurried by, a rush that was now a slow trot as she approached the head of the stairs. Suddenly, she stopped, one hand pressed tightly against her stomach. Standing at the foot of the staircase was Ambrose Toal, speaking softly to a shorter, stouter man whose last vestige of hair was confined to puffed fringes above his ears. It was Simon Bains, and Natalie knew instinctively that this would be the wrong moment to be seen by either of them. She made a quick about-face and strode along the thick carpet, the purse a dead weight in her hand, her neck protesting as she jerked hurried looks at each passing doorway. At corridor's end she paused, looked back over her shoulder and saw the two men just coming to the landing. At the same time, the door to the powder room opened and

Christine and Cynthia stepped out, arm in arm. And smiling.

Without thinking, Natalie ducked into the rear hallway and pressed herself against the wall. The only light was a dimly yellow glow from the center hall. You should have tried a bluff, she scolded herself, and prayed for a warning of the quartet's approach. She was rewarded a moment later by Cynthia's low, manlike laughter. They were headed in her direction.

Nearly stumbling in her haste, Natalie felt her way along the wall, trying each door in passing, more frantically as the voices grew louder. Suddenly one gave way and she darted inside, pushing it silently closed behind her. Here there were no windows, nor switches close at hand, and she was forced to press an ear against the thick wood, listening, hearing Christine snap something and a man respond angrily.

Talk about insane, she thought as she waited until she could be positive they had left her alone. I don't believe this is happening to me. I really don't believe it.

The room's darkness was complete. With her back pressed against the door, she tried to create images of the furniture she sensed was in her way. Her legs began to weaken, betraying the relief she felt, and her breasts rubbed roughly against the caftan as she swallowed the stifling, musty air. The hair at the back of her neck tingled, and her skin tightened. Electricity, she thought, but couldn't fathom the source. A thought, and she bent to peer through the keyhole, but it was blocked, and she straightened, one hand rubbing her cheek.

All right, then, do I wait or plunge back out?

Discretion, she decided a moment later, but she was determined not to spend the time blind. Damning herself for quitting smoking and not having matches, she inched sideways past the door. Her hand darted over the wall—paneling by the feel of it—and she was about to despair when her thumb triggered a switch and she was sighted again.

The room was larger than she'd imagined, and nothing she'd seen downstairs prepared her for its starkness. Except for a pale blue runner along the baseboard, the floor was bare and painted a glossy black. The single light came from a bulb placed in a topless brass censor that had been lowered from the ceiling on a braided black chain. Three walls were covered by midnight-green velvet, her wall by a walnut veneer polished to near mirror perfection. There were no chairs or tables; nothing at all but the light, the snakelike shadow of the chain, and the floor that reminded her of deep winter ice on a mountain lake.

Her immediate impressions centered on a chamber of the occult. The popularity of Satanism and its attendant offspring had given her ample opportunity to browse through the library's growing collection on the subject, and here there was nothing vaguely similar to anything she had come across. Then, for no clear reason, she thought: meditation! The bare flooring for discomfort, the velvet to swallow sound. She raised her eyebrows in grudging acceptance—Mr. Toal, she decided, was a man of several interests.

A muffled voice panicked her into dousing the light.

Nothing.

Be cool, Natalie, she ordered. You're scaring yourself to death.

And in the darkness, the afterimage of the room persisted until she felt an irrational sensation of imminent suffocation.

Out, then, and her hand closed around the glass doorknob. It turned, though not smoothly, and she pulled the heavy wood to her as cautiously as she could. The first glimpse of the dim hall light temporarily blinded her, but in listening, she heard nothing; no footsteps, no argument. Then: The faint thumping of drums from below, and the strident punctuation of laughter above the hum of conversation. A ritual in a hive, she thought and increased the opening sufficient to allow her head to poke through. The hall was deserted, and without waiting to see if there were signs of impending company, she slid out, closed the door behind her and ran to the main corridor. Lucky you, she told herself as she passed the powder room, then slowed to what she hoped would be a natural, casually bored walk.

Another moment of caution when she reached the bannister and quickly surveyed the entrance hall. Except for the servant still in his place by the door, it too was empty, and it was all she could do to keep from laughing as she descended, one hand sliding along the waxed wood, the other holding her purse loosely at her side.

"A queen, and a pity these aren't marble, either."

Her heart raced, but her face was passive as she glanced over the railing and saw Marc sitting on a bench. He had a glass in his hand and was toasting her with a broad smile. When she joined him, he offered her a drink and she accepted it gladly.

"Having a wonderful evening?"

"Lovely," she said, but stopped short of telling him what had just happened, what she had overheard.

"What?" he asked, sensing her indecision. When she shook her head, he set the glass on the floor and stood over her. "What do you say we truck out of here, as Dederson would say? I've got my words of wisdom from the man, and you look as though you could stand a little depressurizing."

"If you're inviting me out to a bar, you're on," she said, rising.

"Do you think Gernard will miss you?"

She considered several appropriately obscene remarks, poked his stomach instead.

"Our coats," he said. "Wait a sec. I'll be back in a flash."

He hurried off and cornered the Pakistani. The servant nodded at his whispering and vanished into a room opposite the buffet entrance.

With her palms beginning to feel uncomfortably moist, Natalie stood by the newel post and was unable to stop herself from gasping when a hand gripped her shoulder.

"Mrs. Windsor," said a man on the stairs. He was in dinner jacket and black tie, with a violet sash diagonally across his chest. His hair was long, white and brushed straight back from a smooth brow. His nose had been broken at least twice, but the cragged angle only served to underscore rather than detract from the out-of-doors ruggedness his profile maintained. In startling contrast, his hand was pale, almost femininely soft. "I don't believe we've met formally."

"A pleasure, Mr. Toal," she said as her composure returned. "But if you don't mind my asking, how did you know my name?"

"I make it a point to know every beautiful woman's name in Oxrun Station," he said. "Besides, I am the President of the Council, you know."

To which I am supposed to reply: I owe you my job, don't I? she thought; but I'll be hanged if I will.

Her silence seemed to disconcert him and he half turned to leave. Then, changing his mind, he leaned forward and whispered as Marc approached, "I am grateful you came tonight, Mrs. Windsor. But you are out of your league, aren't you?"

"League? I didn't know we were playing baseball, Mr. Toal."

He glared at her quip, and released her shoulder. He nodded curtly at Marc and brushed past him into the reception room.

"Well," Marc said. "You two make friends?"

Natalie chewed thoughtfully at her lower lip.

"No, but I think I've just been threatened."

Chapter 4

THE CHANCELLOR Inn had once been the residence of a prosperous Oxrun farmer who had died during an abolitionist riot in Hartford prior to the Civil War. And whatever he might actually have been like during his lifetime, the huge, dark-hued oil hanging over the fireplace in the main lounge portrayed him as a rugged, no-nonsense individual who would just as soon thrash his opponents as compromise with them. The present owner, Artemus Hall, attributed the generally subdued atmosphere of his Inn's second floor salon to the portrait's glaring black eyes rather than the indirect lighting. In contrast to the rest of the building, there were no tables, the clientele being restricted to small booths thickly leathered with highly polished armrests wide enough for drink and limb. Between the booths were pewter ash trays and broad-topped pedestals on which were centered candles under red chimneys. And although the conversations were suitably lowered and carefully interwoven with unobtrusive taped music, there was no intrusion at all from the larger, noisier restaurant below.

When Natalie and Marc arrived, still shivering from the bitter night air, the only booth available was in the back corner and partially hidden by the fireplace's protruding fieldstone side.

"Cosy," Natalie said as a waitress took their overcoats. Marc exaggerated stumbling through the dim light, and she sighed. He was not the most romantic man in the world. But she kept silent when he ordered for both of them, lighted a cigarette and leaned back against the gleaming leather.

"I'm always waiting for Aaron Burr to walk in," he said, "looking for a clear shot at Hamilton. Or some plantation owner a-busting in demanding we turn over his runaway slave or be hanged in the trying."

"Lovely thought," she said, accepting her sour from the offered tray. She sipped it gratefully. A double, no ice, and the foam stuck to and sweetened her upper lip. "But what's the matter with Washington?"

"In a room like this? This," he said with a deep voice and conspiratorial frown, "is the room for intrigue, my dear, not patriotism or flags flying over Trenton on Christmas Day. Aaron Burr, Simon Legree, or perhaps even Benny Arnold skulking in from black deeds at

West Point. We in the know always call him Benny, you see."

She smiled, sipped again, and finally allowed herself to relax. The cowl bunched uncomfortably against her back, but she ignored it; a penance for the presumption of the costume, she thought.

"Now," he said after they'd had their first drink in easy silence and had ordered another round, "what's all this about a threat from our leading money-changer?"

The time had been long in coming. It was one thing for her to maintain a solitary existence in a town not noted for leaving its more notorious citizenry alone—it was, in fact, relatively easy and she'd few complaints. The mourning for Ben had ended; less than a year with him was not the most solid foundation for a lifetime of black and blue shadows under one's eyes. She had just wanted to be alone, and her weapon was the acceptable aloofness her widowhood perpetuated. However, it was quite another thing to keep her own counsel in matters that were beginning to instill in her a nebulous dread. Had she mentioned this to Sam, Miriam, or Elaine, she knew she would have been tolerated, jollied, tsked at and patted figuratively on the head with admonitions to take a vacation, that the books in the stacks were becoming too real; what she needed was a human—male—companion to show her the way back into the real world.

And immediately she'd become acquainted

with Marc, she had hoped he would brush all that nonsense aside and make himself available for a little old-fashioned shoulder crying.

Yet she hesitated under his patient stare.

Suppose, she thought, his shoulder wasn't broad enough?

Then he shifted and lighted a second cigarette from the candle. When the waitress glared at him, he threw her a kiss, blew her a smoke ring and sat back to wait.

She told him, repeating the overheard conversation almost verbatim, hissing the remarks Toal had made while she'd been standing by the staircase. He said nothing, toying with his glass instead, using the swizzle stick to spear at the cherry and orange slice. Finally, as she finished, he gave her a small boy look of apology and used a finger to slide out the fruit and pop them into his mouth. His lips puckered and he sucked in air sharply.

"My teeth are going to rot," he said, signaling for a refill. "One should never make a sour with Southern Comfort instead of whiskey—it does decadent things to one's brain."

It was an effort not to shout at him.

"He really said that?"

She nodded, watched him light still another cigarette. The match's flame added lines to his face, and the candle in the red chimney reflected its own light in his glasses. As he tilted his head, the flame centered itself in the lenses, and she shuddered and pushed the chimney aside.

"Well, I'll tell you, girl, I think our Mr. Toal is a very strange person. Peculiar strange, I mean. And if I had the slightest idea what he meant, or what his wife and barracuda daughter meant, I'd be the first to tell you."

"You don't like Cynthia?"

"Who, me? Just because a couple of months ago, out of the clear blue whatever, she tried to rape me in the office, then followed me around like a bitch in heat for three weeks— why should I not like her?" He frowned then. "I'll never understand that. I'd only met her once before, at something Dederson was throwing at the paper. He introduced us, in fact." He grinned. "Not that I want to make a connection, but things haven't been the same at the old press since."

A quick and inexplicable moment of anger was followed instantly by a decision. "Marc, let me tell you something else."

He nodded, once, Cynthia already forgotten.

"You remember those papers I was working on when you picked me up tonight?"

"I resent the phrase 'picked you up.' It implies salacious consent on your part."

"To know me is to pick me," she said. "Now will you please listen for a minute?"

He tried a lecherous grin and, laughing at her expression, crossed his knees and began tracing patterns in the moisture left by his glass on the arm rest.

"Every so often, the Council—which is my ultimate collective employer—asks Mrs. Hall about the books we order. But only every so often. We've never been told not to buy anything, nor have we ever been overruled on orders already a *fait accompli*. What they ask is which books have been taken out the most, which ones seem to be a waste of town money."

"Reasonable," he muttered, not really interrupting.

"Absolutely," she said, "and thanks to the college's computer, all I have to do is request the information and I get a complete run-through of the frequency of usage for every volume in the library. Once I pass that on to the Council, I never hear about it again. At least, I never heard from them before."

"But then?"

"But then, last June—no, last May, it was—they wanted to establish a system of prior approval for all the books we purchased, with the proviso that they could add or delete books of their own if they wanted."

A woman on the far side of the fireplace suddenly burst into laughter, too loud to be completely sober. The booth's back was too high for Natalie to see her, but a moment after the disturbance began she saw the emaciated shadow of Artemus Hall threading his way solemnly across the floor. A sharp whispered exchange resulted in a couple striding quickly out, their dignity faltering by the pursuit of the innkeeper's shadow. It all happened so quickly, there weren't half a dozen ripples to mark the incident's passing.

Natalie shook her head. Sympathy for the embarrassment. Disgust for the forgetfulness that allowed people to get drunk. She looked at Marc, watched him tap his swizzle stick lightly against the rim of the ash tray. He cleared his throat.

"I, uh, can see where this would get you upset, Nat, what with your sovereignty not stepped on before. But they're still within their rights, you know. He who holds the purse strings and all that crap."

"That's not what bothers me," she said. "You see, ever since this system started, books have been missing from the stacks. Not the usual and expected losses you get from kids and a few sticky-fingered cheapskates. Odd books, books you'd never think somebody would want to steal."

"Like what?"

"Well," and she dropped her hands into her lap and rubbed one thumb against the other, "first of all, those that usually go are the current best sellers, or the reference books that cost a small fortune if you buy them in the store. Now, almost every Bible in the place has been taken. A couple of Books of Mormon, a Koran, a pair of specially bound Pentateuchs. All of them gone."

"Religious fanatic," he suggested. "Somebody who hates God?"

She shrugged. "I thought so, at first. But

then there are the nonfictional inspirational types, all of them, too."

"Atheist, then, who can't even stand the secular religions."

Natalie grinned, and forced herself to relax as soon as she realized how stiff she'd been holding herself. Marc was following directly along the trail she herself had taken when she'd winnowed from the inventory the list of stolen books. "Then how do you explain Nietzsche, Kant, Spinoza, and a dozen more like them? Or Darwin, Sagan, even the most modern types of mysteries and science fiction?"

He rubbed a hand over his face, emptied his glass and waved off the waitress when she made a pass for it. He smoked another cigarette halfway to the filter before lifting his palms in surrender. "All right, I can't make the connection. What do you have?"

"Nothing, really," she said truthfully. "Not yet, anyway. But when I asked Mrs. Hall about the thefts, she nearly hit the ceiling. It was strange, Marc, really strange."

Mrs. Windsor, I thought your duties had been made quite plain to you?

Really, Mrs. Hall, I only wanted to tell you about a situation you should be aware of. These stolen books—

Mrs. Windsor, you are trying my patience. I was led to believe that you were reasonably experienced in library administration. A college graduate, isn't that right? Didn't they teach you about inventory losses? Don't you know there are children who love—

To steal Spinoza? Come on, Mrs. Hall, really!

Natalie, Natalie, you're making too much of a perfectly ordinary situation. We have to expect—yes, even in a place like Oxrun Station—we have to expect a certain amount of thievery to go on in any given year. It's even included in the budget, Natalie, as I'm sure you are well aware of.

But there are so many!

Natalie, I haven't time to argue with you, not time enough to teach you what you should already know. Please forget it.

Mrs. Hall, there's no need to get—

Mrs. Windsor, for the last time, I'm asking you to forget this matter. And if it comes down to it, this is not your province as defined by your contract. I will take care of it, as always.

Wouldn't you like some help, though? There's so much to do.

Mrs. Windsor . . . Natalie . . . I am trying to be pleasant and you're not helping me a bit by pursuing something that is, frankly, none of your business. You still have a great deal to learn about the tasks you're already supposed to be performing. I do not want you taking on something else. Your own duties, Mrs. Windsor, or . . .

Or what, Mrs. Hall?

You're a librarian, Mrs. Windsor . . . read between the lines.

Natalie's face flushed with anger. "Naturally, that didn't stop me. And that's when I found out the other thing."

"Lord, woman, are you Ellery Queen in drag?"

"You'll never know," she said, knowing there was a blush at her neck in reaction to his staring admiration. "Look, let's go back to the library. I want you to see what I was doing, see if you come to the same conclusion I did."

"Which is?"

She waved the query aside brusquely. "No fair. I don't want to prejudice the witness."

"Whatever you say, madam detective. The chariot awaits without."

"The way you drive, without gas, most likely."

"You," he said, "are a kill-joy."

The narrow parking lot behind the library was dimly lighted, a measure that received the strong and futile disapproval of the staff in the wake of an energy-saving program initiated the previous spring. It was reasonable, the Council argued, to suppose that since the library was closed for long stretches at a time, there was no need to light the parking lot for anybody. Criminals, they added in anticipation of protests, would get in no matter what. Darkness would force them to be more careful and therefore less likely to smash glass and damage doors.

It was the kind of reasoning that often made Natalie wish she had taken up steel work or coal mining.

They decided to use the side entrance rather than call undue attention to themselves by going in the front way. Should a passing patrol see the light at the desk or in her office window, they would not as a rule investigate because there were few on the force, thanks to Sam, who didn't know her erratic working hours. She whispered this to Marc while she fumbled with her passkey; then she took a deep breath and pulled him inside.

They were in a narrow corridor that ended abruptly behind them. The floor sloped gently upward toward the front, and they had gone only a few paces before Natalie froze, one hand clutching an aluminum bannister, the other Marc's arm. He started to speak but she placed a hand quickly against his mouth and listened.

Silence.

Night chill.

An occasional creak as the afternoon warmth escaped into darkness.

She felt his lips brush her ear.

"What?"

She shook her head, realized he couldn't see her and leaned closer. Both hands now clamped his arm tightly. "I think I heard something."

"Not me. Not a thing."

"I did. I'm sure of it."

Silence again, and the distant sound of a passing truck.

"Vandals?"

"I don't know. Maybe."

"You lead the way. I'll kill myself bumping into tables."

He rested his fingers lightly against her waist as she moved cautiously up and into the main room. Here the street lights dispersed the darkness into a deep winter's dusk, and the shadowed bulk of racks and cases loomed and threatened. A chair scraped against a table when her hip struck it. There was a whispered curse when Marc trod on her heel and stumbled into the wall they were following.

Natalie pulled at the rope at her waist. Grabbed at the tassel and rolled it nervously between her fingers. She couldn't rid herself of the feeling that there was more than just the two of them in the building. And something else. A tension she knew was outside the fact of her after-hours prowling. She sniffed once, instantly sorting out the traces of books, wax, carpeting, the evening itself. Nothing unusual, nothing exotic. She rubbed palm over wrist. Pushed the hand up her oversized sleeve: the hairs on her arm were bristling.

Static electricity.

Not from the floor. In the air. And a closeness that reminded her fleetingly of being in a cavern miles below the surface of the ground.

"The lights," Marc whispered, and she yelped, slapped a hand over her mouth and leaned weakly against him. There was then a surging temptation to lash out at him for frightening her, but he had already moved away and suddenly she was blinded by a tower of white light in the center of the huge room. The chandelier glared, dimmed as Marc turned the dial, and she rubbed her eyes before rushing to the countered desk.

Marc darted toward the stacks and began poking into the shadows.

"Forget it," she called finally. "Whoever was here is probably gone by now."

"How can you be sure?"

"They got what they wanted. Look."

As he rushed back, she pointed to the broad counter. There were several manila folders scattered and opened on the white-and-blue formica. Most contained the copies of invoices shuffled hopelessly out of order. While Marc leafed through them, she hurried around to the horseshoe's open end and pulled a key from her purse. The cash drawer seemed undisturbed, but when she pulled it to her the printout and all her typing was missing.

She reached behind her and pulled the chair to her knees. She sat heavily. Though she had been sure something was happening in the system without her knowledge, there had still been a glimmering hope that its importance had been exaggerated. The burglary, however, emphatically denied it.

"Those things you put in before," Marc said. "Gone, right?"

She looked up into the concern on his face. A breath, and she nodded.

"I was looking for a pattern, Marc. I'd only been guessing before, but now I'm sure that every time the Council put in an order of its own, the same number of books always managed to disappear before the month was up. Every time, Marc. Every time since last June."

"Now that doesn't make any sense."

Natalie slapped her hands on the counter and pulled herself to her feet. "I know it doesn't make any sense, Marc. I know it. But the fact remains: I've learned what's going on around here, and now all the evidence I had has been stolen."

His startled look lasted only a fraction of a second. "Now, hold on, Nat. You can always request another print run, can't you? I mean, all it would take is a telephone call on Monday, right?"

She considered, and nodded. Reluctantly. "But I'll bet you a week's pay there's suddenly something wrong with the system, or the cost of runs has become too expensive and needs Mrs. Hall's approval, or something like that. I'll bet you I can't get another list like that unless I do it myself. By hand."

"Which would take you . . ."

For an answer she gestured dramatically toward all the bookcases and stacks.

"A problem," he said, and she closed her eyes in weary agreement.

Tension returned.

She opened her eyes and was swept by the sensation that she was floating aimlessly beneath the surface of a grey motionless sea, and all her gestures took minutes instead of seconds to complete. She tried to count how many drinks she had had that night. Two or three at the mansion, at least two at the Inn, and whatever had been in them was not mixing well. She passed a hand over her damp forehead and looked over the counter, aware that Marc was speaking to her but she was unable to hear or understand him. She smiled weakly, then laughed at the comical twist his lips had taken as they groped for words. Another laugh when he reached out for her hand and a glaring red lightning bolt leaped painlessly between the tips of her fingers. She floated a hand over the invoices and saw them flutter like birds disturbed in their sleep. Without warning, her stomach wrenched and she grabbed at it, reached out a hand to brace herself against the desk.

"Marc!" she managed to gasp, and watched helplessly as he sprawled over the counter and slid slowly out of sight to the floor. The folders tipped after him. Slowly.

A tear etched into her cheek. She released the counter to wipe it away, swayed and stumbled backward, spun around and grabbed for the chair. It skittered away. She fell. Landed on her shoulder, toppled to her back while the ceiling whirled above her, the chandelier swinging in time to an inaudible tune.

Voices, then.

A whispering.

Little children sneaking fearfully through a haunted house in the wake of midnight.

Prowlers directing their energies at a stubborn massive safe.

A higher pitch, and it was the push of dead leaves along a deserted sidewalk. Scraping. Rustling. A brittle and lonely scratching for purchase.

Shaking her head, Natalie propped herself up on her elbows. She gathered her legs under her, tipped herself forward and grabbed at one of the shelves under the counter. Pulled. Knelt. Her arms reached up and she hauled, was standing.

"Marc?"

Lost. In a cavern without echoes. Directly beneath the glaring white light, blind to what hovered at its fringes.

"Marc, are you all right?"

The front doors shattered inward. Her mouth opened for a scream, but there was no sound. Shards of glass tumbled end over end across the carpeting, tinkled on the tables and racks like wind chimes too heavy to be musical. She tried to duck away from the knifelike missiles, but they struck her mercilessly, blunt nails that punctured her arms, cheeks, forehead, palms. Drawing globules of blood that gathered like red mercury and splashed to the papers on the counter. The stains spread, the pain spread, and still the glass rained in from the doors.

And there was no wind.

Finally, the scream found its way out, and she pressed her bleeding hands to her face to protect her eyes. Whirling, stumbling over the fallen chair, spinning to regain her balance and fleeing toward the stacks. She tripped over a writhing pool of magazines and nearly lost consciousness when her hands struck the floor and drove the glass deeper into her skin.

She was going to bleed to death. She was going to die slowly, under a shroud of drifting pink.

Windsound.

A billowing hand of dust that clouded the light, a manic shrieking that ripped over her screams. The books flew from the shelves like leaves before a storm, thudding off her shoulders, back, striking and falling from her head. She rose, ran, tripped over a dictionary. Her sandals were torn from her feet and instantly glass embedded itself in her soles. She threw up her arms to cover her face and the shelves emptied around her, buried her to her neck, pinned her to the floor.

A spark. A charge. A bolt that multiplied and sucked the air from her lungs.

Though she knew it was impossible, she could see a figure standing in the demolished doorway. Neither man nor woman, it waited until the turmoil had subsided. It approached, a shimmering black edged in fingers of electric discharge. Clamping her eyes shut, Natalie waited, sensing. Something shoved her head to one side, and there was a brief lance of pain by her right temple.

She was deaf, and when she opened her eyes, the severed ear hovered by her mouth.

Darkness, and beneath it a quiescent nausea no longer threatening. Natalie breathed deeply several times, clenched her fists at her sides and opened her eyes. The chandelier had been extinguished, a tiny gooseneck lamp on the counter a poor imitation. She was lying next to the chair, and a shadow knelt beside her, taking up her hands and muttering what sounded like incantations. When it saw her staring, it reached up and lifted the lamp to the floor.

"Oh, my God, Marc," she said, and suddenly slapped a hand to the side of her head. Then she yanked it away and stared. There were no sounds, no blood, no intimations of either. Despite Marc's protests, then, she pushed herself to a sitting position and twisted around. The floor was clean; the books were on their shelves, the magazines in their racks.

"Marc?"

He shifted to sit squarely on the floor and

began chafing her wrists while searching her face for signs of illness, or hysteria. "One of us," he said, "had better learn what drinks mix with what drinks, and what drinks one must never ever combine with another. God Almighty, lady, I thought you were going to die on me, and me with no excuse for being in here except for the invitation of a swizzled librarian."

Dizziness clouded over her until she lowered her head to his shoulder. "I don't think . . ."

"What? What don't you think, lady?"

"I don't think it was the drinks, Marc."

"What was? Your passing out?"

She wanted to lift her head again, to scan the lines of his face, touch the corners of his mouth as if this would serve to clear her mind. Fainting, the nausea, this she could easily reconcile from having too much on an empty stomach. But she could not find a reason for the dreams, the hallucinations. She reached a hand to his chin and pinched it carefully, feeling the cool skin contract and the perceptible stubble of a beard. He stroked her long hair, bunched it in a fist and tugged gently.

"You're a secret drinker, lady. I never would have thought it of you."

"I'm not," she protested. "It . . . it took so long."

"What long? A couple of minutes at the most. You keeled over right after that spark thing. You know, static electricity in the rug. We touched, you jumped and passed out."

"You didn't see anything? Anything at all?"

His lips were close to her ear, and the air from his mouth as he spoke tickled.

"All I saw was you dive bombing to the floor, lady. You nearly cracked your head open on that chair."

She trembled violently, and his arm tightened. She opened her mouth, and closed it instantly. It would do no good now to tell him what she'd seen. He would only say it was the drinks, the excitement of the party and the theft. He would tell her in that maddeningly persuasive manner that Vorhees' murder had triggered an unpleasant memory, that she was keeping her fears bottled inside and the liquor only served to break down the barrier. A psychic nightmare, and nothing more.

That's what he would tell her, and she would believe him if she listened.

Because he was probably right.

On the countertop she saw an invoice flutter.

"Is there a door open?"

"Hey, relax," he said, helping her to her feet. "There's nothing to be afraid of. It was so close in here I had to open it to get you some air."

Immediately aware of the chill that crept under her dress, she hugged herself.

"Now, I suggest we get you home and into

bed. Your head is going to have to answer a lot of questions in the morning, you know. I have some remedies I'll tell you about on the way back."

"But the papers . . ."

"Oh." He released her and leaned on the counter, toying with one of the invoices. "Well, I guess we could call the cops."

But he sounded doubtful, and Natalie understood. If they called the police and reported the theft, they would have to try to explain why the papers were important; and for the time being, they were nothing more than a puzzling suspicion. She knew there was no crime in replacing lost books, no question of funds being misappropriated. And the Council would hear about it, and there would go her job.

"Who?" she suddenly demanded of the library. "Who took them?"

Marc shrugged, then stiffened and placed a hand at the small of her back. A man was standing in the entrance, a flashlight in his hand. Behind him they could see the winking red light atop a patrol car.

"It's only me, officer," she called out, hoping she sounded braver than she felt. "It's Natalie Windsor. I just had some checking to do. You know how it is with me."

The patrolman stepped into the library, darting his light into the corners. "Saw the light on, Mrs. Windsor, and the door open." His voice was flat, not bothering to seem official, just skeptical. "Just thought I'd check. Orders, you know, since last night."

It was supposed to have been an apology. Natalie, however, didn't care. Her eyes had developed a light, persistent stinging, and her arms became heavy and hung limply at her sides.

Sensing her exhaustion, Marc guided her around the front desk and past the officer into the open air. He pulled the caftan's cowl into a collar at her neck, waved to the patrolman and took her around to the parking lot.

"I'll take you home," he said as he helped her into the car and draped her coat over her shoulders. "Then, if you don't mind, I'll drive myself home. I'll bring this heap back in the morning."

"Don't you dare," she said. "In the afternoon. I expect to be dead until at least twelve."

As they backed into the street, she suddenly remembered the lamp on the floor. Nuts, she thought. Let the fatheads pay.

At the corner she glanced toward the library and saw the patrol car still at the curb. The policeman was standing by the hood, staring after them.

He was holding the radio mike in his cupped hand.

Chapter 5

BY THE time Natalie had crawled into bed the following night, she was ready to believe the day had been some diabolical reincarnation of a Friday the Thirteenth wrenched from the most dismal December on record.

Despite the previous day's golden autumn promise, Sunday morning had retreated abruptly under cover of a light rain that had gradually thickened to a windless monotonous downpour. She had awakened past ten, had stayed under the tufted quilt to watch as the world drowned under skittering droplets on the pane. The dampness, the grey, and an almost summerlike lassitude kept her from dressing immediately and turned the bed into a cocoon of nearly sinful warmth.

Her sleep had been dreamless, her head clear when she finally opened her eyes, and it was an unpleasant moment of disorientation before she remembered Saturday. It was, then, a perverse situation, welcome but somewhat inexplicable. She thought there should have been nightmares to drench her in sweat, to force her to pace through the empty house in search of respite and comforting rationalizations. Or, at the very least, confused and uncertain struggles with an illusory Marc; there should have been something of an attempt to define the parameters of their relationship, to gauge the intensity of her fluctuating and mist-covered emotions.

But there had been nothing. Not even a headache in penance for her drinking.

And the rain limited the options of a day's activities.

So she had stayed in bed until noon, punching her pillow, thrashing to locate a comfortable position while she tried to make sense out of what was apparently senseless.

Mrs. Toal and Cynthia arguing: about her? In retrospect, it was very nearly laughable. Why should they be? Natalie had seen but a few of the dozens of guests at the reception, and any number of women, including Miriam, could easily have fit the description "wearing a nightgown." Simple enough. She had panicked because she'd been eavesdropping; at times, guilt was a remarkable equalizer. And Toal's remark was merely a distinction between his status and hers—the breeding, he was telling her, that instant wealth brings; in a democratic society, the dollar decides the class. And she was, after all, only an assistant librarian.

The library. That she had already worked out before she'd even left the building.

And the books. Was it really that much of a surprise that they were replaced? Did she really believe that despite the Director's expertise in the field she herself was the only one there who knew how to read the best-seller lists? Were there something to the Council's peremptory manner, Adriana would have informed her. She would have. The fact that she hadn't was neither suspicious nor unkind. It was, Natalie decided, simply one of those so-called executive decisions that she knew she needed to keep her in her place.

It was true. Often, she thought herself the leader and the staff merely the rest of the troops. It was a spanking, she told herself. Nothing but a spanking.

The debates and answers had ended when her shoulders and back started to ache. She sighed and indulged herself in a thirty-minute shower. The water had been hot enough to pinken the Mediterranean cast of her skin, and the towel rough enough to make her gasp as she rubbed it briskly over small breasts, flat stomach, adolescently slim thighs. Dutifully, then, she sat in front of the mirror and brushed her hair its hundred strokes, leaned on her elbows and mentally banished the sharp bite of the tweezers while she plucked her eyebrows and wished the thin look weren't so damned fashionable.

Through breakfast, she'd thought of Marc

and the touch of his hand on her arm, the small of her back, the brush of his lips across her ear in the darkened library—and the way he had waited patiently on the front porch until she was inside and had switched on the hall light. The kiss at the door—schoolboy light—that lingered long after the taillights of her car had vanished around the corner. He had returned just after she'd finished a tasteless lunch, and stayed only long enough to joke about his hangover and leave the number of the hotel he would be using in New York for the next four days.

"Dederson's decided he owes me after that debacle last night," he said. "Seems there's a big-deal financial meeting in the city this week, and he doesn't trust the wire services. What with all the money that floats around the Station, he wants his man on the scene at all times to give us the straight scoop." He grinned and shook his head. "Straight scoop. Another memorable quote from our with-it publisher."

She'd folded the paper carefully and slipped it into her bathrobe pocket.

"In case you need a little help in your pursuits," he'd said, and she'd been surprised at the disappointment in his face when she explained the conclusions she'd come to in bed. "Oh, well, I was kind of hoping we'd have a little mystery . . ." He waved his hand and had turned to the door. "Never mind. Just keep the number anyway. Just in case."

When he'd left, the house became discouragingly larger, and the room in each of its corners too large for her to enjoy. She'd read chapters from several books, leafed uninterestedly through the Sunday paper, and when the television programs began to put her to sleep, she'd surrendered and blackened the house.

What a waste, she thought as she lay stiffly in the darkness.

The rain, having drummed steadily throughout the day, was virtually silent, and still there was no wind to shatter it against the windows. The rain, the day, the books, even her thoughts were all dull. And the disappointment that she felt in no longer being threatened by something she'd been trying to find—something that obviously wasn't there—was a tangible weight on her chest, and kept her awake long after midnight.

"I know what day it is," she said sharply, tapping a finger angrily against the Wednesday sheet on her desk calendar. "I am not a cretin, you know."

The middle-aged woman sitting primly opposite her desk drew her thick lips taut and puffed her overweight frame. She was wearing a worn cloth overcoat that hung unflatteringly to the tops of her tie shoes, shoes so small her feet were forced to swell and bulge over the sides. In every respect porcine, Natalie thought uncharitably, even to the thin dark moustachelike bristles on her upper lip.

"Well, you could have at least called, Nattie. I've been so worried about you; and you insist on not answering your telephone."

Natalie sighed the cry of a martyr. "Elaine, I have been busy, and tired, and I really don't know why I should have to check in with you every other day."

Elaine Windsor smiled tolerantly. "It's not checking in, dear. Sam and I just care about you, that's all. And besides, you weren't too tired to go to the Inn last night."

Last night. The house had become too small, too cramped, and without knowing why, she'd driven to the Chancellor Inn and sat alone in an upstairs booth. She'd had a Comfort sour, a few minutes of polite banter with Artemus Hall, and a careful ride home feeling oddly incomplete.

"I . . ." And she decided again there had to be parts of her life, and preferably all of it, that Elaine was not privy to. "What can I do for you, Elaine?" she said stiffly, making a rude show of checking her watch. "I have a meeting with Mrs. Hall in a few minutes, and I don't want to be late."

Elaine fussed with a tissue in her pocketbook, sniffed once and rose. "I just wanted you to know that if you need any help, we are always around. We are your friends, Nattie," she said, suddenly leaning over the desk, her eyes dark extensions of the puffiness beneath them. "We want to help you."

She hesitated then, and Natalie frowned, curious in spite of her revulsion for the woman's prying. She managed a quick encouraging smile, and Elaine beamed as though delivered a victory. "I heard you were mixing it up with the biggies last weekend." Her expression was conspiratorial, and for a moment Natalie thought all she wanted was gossip for her friends. "You were there with that reporter fellow from the *Herald*, right?"

"My heavens," Natalie said, just barely keeping the bitterness out of her voice, "it seems like I'm the subject for a documentary or something. Don't tell me you were following me around all that time, dear?"

Elaine laughed, and Natalie turned to look out the side window.

"Oh, my heavens, no. But I do have my sources, you know." She paused. "I surely do." Another moment, and Natalie bit her lips to keep from smiling. "I just wondered if there might be a little something going on between you two. You know what I mean."

It was then that she found the key to a portion of the restlessness that had dogged her over the past few months: No, she thought, there was nothing definite between her and Marc, and that, she scowled, was the trouble!

"Elaine," she said as she came round the desk and ushered her to the door, "I really do have a meeting, and I wish you wouldn't worry so much. If anything comes up in the romance line, you'll be the first to know."

They stood at the gallery railing and looked

down at the main floor. Elaine nodded, then squeezed Natalie's hand and left. Miriam, looking up from the desk, puffed her cheeks and tapped a finger to her temple. Natalie laughed, waved and turned as the Director's door swung open.

"Your company gone, Natalie?"

Adriana Hall was virtually the same size with the same figure as Natalie, yet her bearing and conscious cultivation of her position made her seem tall, slender, and in every way the matriarch of a going concern.

"My late husband's sister-in-law," she said. "She worries about me even though I'm not in the family anymore."

"As do we all, dear, as do we all." She pulled a small watch from her tightly restrained bosom and glanced pointedly at it. "I think it's time for our meeting. Shall we?" And she stepped aside to allow Natalie first entrance.

The office was a direct and overpowering contrast to her own, and Natalie instantly felt like a girl quivering in front of the principal's desk. Walnut and silver plaques dotted the pale green walls, a scroll from Harvard prominently centered; a thickly upholstered chair and matching divan, oval ebony desk studiously littered with letterheads and envelopes, a cabinet on top of which was a silver service, decanter and siphon. The window overlooked the small park beyond the parking lot, and the light was diffused a gentle autumn yellow.

Adriana moved slowly to her chair and waved Natalie to the divan. "The others," she said to Natalie's glance at the closed door, "won't be here. I felt a short upper-level conference was in order, if you don't mind."

Natalie immediately shook her head and forced her hands to remain resting on her knees rather than cringing in her lap.

"I didn't bring this up Monday, Natalie, because I thought the timing would be inappropriate. But I have a report from the police that you and . . . and . . ."

"Clayton. Marcus Clayton."

"Yes, Marcus Clayton. Well, I understand that you and this Mr. Clayton were here rather late this past Saturday evening."

The decision to lie was made without thought. "Yes," she said. "We were going for a drive. We passed the library and I saw a light on and I was sure I'd turned them all off when I left. I went in with my passkey and turned it off."

Adriana picked up a fountain pen from a stand at the front of the desk and rolled it slowly between her fingers. "The patrolman who interrupted you—"

"There was nothing to interrupt."

"—said the light had been on for some time."

"So? We went in the side door. He couldn't see us through the dark glass, probably. I'd had a little too much to drink, you see, and felt a bit dizzy. I sat at the front desk for a minute." She shrugged, smiling as innocently as she could. "There was, as I said, nothing to interrupt. Surely you know me better than that, Mrs. Hall."

The Director's hesitation was just long enough to be infuriating. "I'm sure, Natalie. But I must have your word that you'll not return to the library after hours without calling me first. The police are nervous lately, as you can well understand."

"Sure thing, Mrs. Hall. I'm sorry if I caused you any trouble." My God, she thought, do you hear me talking, Natalie? Do you really hear this?

"No trouble. None at all." She reached into a drawer and pulled out a red-tagged folder. "This is the purchase order for December. Please take care of it, will you? I still have a dreadful head cold, and my brain refuses to function for more than five minutes at a time."

Natalie rose, took the papers and backed toward the door.

"Oh, and one other thing. There's been a foul-up at the college again, I'm afraid. It looks like we'll have to do without the services of our computer time for the next few days. Would you remember to give a call to whatshisname long about Friday and see when he can get us back in?"

"I'll make a note of it, Mrs. Hall. And why don't you go home and lie down?" She hoped her smile was solicitous. "The air around here isn't exactly fresh, you know."

Adriana placed her long fingers to her brow and nodded. "I think you have struck upon the proper formula, Natalie. Just a little more here and then I'll go. Will you be locking up tonight?"

"Of course. No problem at all." She opened the door, paused at the threshold. "And Mrs. Hall, I really am sorry about Saturday night. I'll be more careful about the lights in the future."

The door closed as the Director swiveled her chair around to face out the window, and the quiet murmuring of the library floor intruded as harshly as a siren. Pressing the folder against her chest, Natalie leaned against the wall and stared at the bronze chain supporting the chandelier. No computer. No chance to double-check to see if she was in fact wondering about nothing at all. The idea that this might be a coincidence lodged weakly and grew until she was calmed: This wasn't the first time the computer link had been disrupted. But there was still the inter- ference in her private life. First Elaine, and now the Director. She thought it finally time she stopped venting her anger over the telephone.

The police station/jail took up most of the Chancellor Avenue frontage between Fox Road and Centre Street. It was a dull marble monument to a long-dead architect who had envisioned law enforcement encased in a pseudo-Grecian temple. The front desk was manned by a sergeant Natalie had never seen, but immediately she entered he reached for an intercom and a moment later Sam Windsor came hurrying down a hall that angled off to the left. He could have been Ben's twin except for the baldness, the ruddy jowls, and the excess weight that pressed tightly against his broad black leather belt.

"Sam, I want to talk to you," Natalie said, her anger stronger, fed by the deliberately slow walk from the library. "Now, if you have the time."

A massive hand hesitated, then clamped loosely onto her arm. "My office, then," he said, and led her back to the hall. He made no attempts at conversation, and she noted instead the people sitting on the wooden benches that lined the freshly painted walls in the corridor. Youngsters, for the most part, sullen and trapped between parents glaring at the portraits of the Presidents spaced between office doors. As they reached Sam's, however, she saw one old man sitting alone. His coat was shredded at the hem, his face unshaven, and a battered and filthy hat twisted endlessly in his trembling hands. He glanced up as they passed and reached out, drew the hand back when Sam glowered. Another drifter, Natalie thought sadly and wondered why they thought Oxrun Station would be any more charitable than the other towns along the highway. This one would be locked up for the night to teach him a lesson, then driven in a patrol car ten miles north or south and released with a warning. It was a distasteful job Ben had done several times, and after each one had threatened to quit.

A man called then, and Sam, muttering apologies, returned to the front to meet a uniformed patrolman carrying a motorcycle helmet under his arm. Natalie took a short step toward Sam's office, stopped and looked back at the drifter. A small smile, and suddenly he was on his feet.

"Miss?"

The voice was low, edged with gravel.

Natalie stepped away from the hand that stretched toward her coat. "I'm sorry," she said with a nervous wave, "but I really don't have any—"

The man flushed a yellow grin and shook his head. "Money? I don't need it, honest. I just want to know what they're going to do with me. I didn't do nothing, you know. Sleeping in that there park is all." The bristled chin dropped toward his chest. "They said I was drunk. Seeing things. Sparkles." He looked up again and she saw the faint yellow tinge behind his red-rimmed eyes. "Don't want to go to jail." He jerked his head toward the others. "Not like them. Don't like jail, you know. Can't get away in jail. Can't be done."

Natalie felt ashamedly helpless, wanting to call out to Sam and at the same time find a word that would comfort the old man's fears. Instead, she groped behind her, turned the knob on Sam's office door and slipped quickly inside.

The office was stark compared to Mrs. Hall's and the clutter here spoke more of Windsor's work habits than the case load. When he returned a second later, she sat in a stiff-backed chair as he perched on the edge of the desk, one booted foot swinging aimlessly.

"Don't worry about that old tramp," he said into the silence. "I heard him shilling you."

"He wasn't asking for money, Sam."

"They never do. They give you the story of their lives and hope it's worth more to you than to them."

"He said something about seeing things in the park."

The foot paused, swung again. "Pink elephants. We found him hiding behind a tree with a stick he was using for a club." He laughed quietly and rolled his eyes toward the ceiling. "I'd just like to know how they get in here."

"Walk, obviously," she said, clipping the words to rebuke his lack of compassion.

A silence, then, and the sounds of the station drifting. A brief scuffling in the corridor. Natalie hoped it wasn't the old man.

"So," Sam said. "You're mad again."

"And you're right again, Sam," she said, one hand at her throat to keep from shouting. "What's the idea of broadcasting my daily schedule all over town?"

"Now, wait a minute—"

"Shut up," she snapped, pleased to see shock fighting the fury in his reddened face. "I am thoroughly sick and tired of all this. What I do with my evenings, mornings, and in my own bed is none of your business, Sam Windsor, and I want you to stop it right now! Today! This minute! You promised me you'd get that patrol off my back—"

"But I did," he protested weakly.

"Maybe so, but your boys on regular duty don't know that. Jesus Christ, Sam—"

"Natalie!" It was more than a shout. It was a parade ground command, and she couldn't help leaning away from its vehemence. "Natalie, you know perfectly well I can't stand that sort of language."

Puzzled, she shook her head. "Since when? The last time we had a fight, you outswore the best of them, if I recall."

"That," he said with a piousness that made her blink, "was swearing. Which is not, I shouldn't have to remind you, the same as blasphemy."

Oh, my God, she thought, the idiot's gotten religion.

"Listen," she said, keeping her voice low to make him lean closer, "all I want is to be left alone. No cops, no cars, nothing special at all. You treat me like you treat everyone else."

"But you're not like everyone else, Nat."

"What? You're nuts, Sam. You're really nuts. Of course I'm just like everyone else. I have no privileges in this town, and I don't want any. And I don't know how I can make it any clearer to you."

"You don't have to." He eased off the desk and straightened his black tie. A sudden glint of gold on his finger made her stare.

"And since when do you belong to a lodge? I thought Elaine was death on that sort of thing."

He blinked uncomprehending until she pointed at his hand. Then he grinned and held the ring out for her inspection. She recognized it instantly. It was an exact copy of the one in the shoe box—a simple gold band with a pair of ruby chips in the center; between them was an almost invisible cut of silver.

"No lodge, see?" He withdrew the hand when she reached out for it. "I remembered Ben's, see, and the other day I just decided I needed a little class. Cops don't ordinarily wear this kind of thing on duty, you know."

"No kidding. But you must take a lot of ribbing."

He grinned and polished the ring against his shirt. "A little, but it helps being the Chief."

"I'll bet," she muttered just loud enough for him to hear. "But what about it, Sam? Will you please let me go?"

He spread his hands wide. "Let you go? Since when have I made you a prisoner?"

She stood, but resisted poking a finger at his chest. "You know what I mean, Sam.

Just let me go, okay? I want your word. Now. Please."

"But Natalie—"

Exasperation closed her eyes, and there was a pounding behind them that made her grimace. "Sam, because of your so-called guardian angel act, I am in big trouble with my boss. I don't have to tell you that I need the money to keep up the house. If I lose this job, I'll have to move elsewhere." She lifted her head and stared up at him. "I don't want to leave, Sam."

"All right," he said finally, and moved behind the desk as though in need of a barrier. "All right. Just don't go and do anything foolish."

"Now what in God's name—"

"Natalie!"

The flush of his cheeks, the narrowing of his eyes forced her back a step. She mumbled an insincere apology and practically ran out of the office. This is insane, she thought, leaning against the wall. I never thought I'd see the day when Sam Windsor would explode at a little cussing.

The old man on the bench was gone. She looked to where he'd been sitting and saw a smudge of dirt on the floor. Your monument, you poor slob, she thought.

And once in the open, brittle air she decided it was time for an extravagance to boost her morale. By the clock on the National Bank on Centre Street, she saw she still had fifteen minutes left on her lunch hour. The reminder made her stomach rumble embarrassingly, but she decided it could wait. First she had to get over the meeting with Sam; secondly, she had to spend a little of her pay check.

A young boy whistled at her. She grinned and startled him by whistling back.

Three sparrows fluttered out of the gutter, wheeled overhead and perched noisily on an awning over the barber shop.

She checked the windows of a dress shop, notions shop, and finally stepped into the understated sparseness of one of the several Centre Street jewelry stores. If nothing else, she thought as she headed for the first display case, the Oxrun rich were wise enough to understand that gems were investments as well as ornaments. It was, in fact, a lesson her own father had taught her long before he himself had had a second minor business collapse into bankruptcy—indirectly, the cause of his death. His entire estate had been fashioned into the blue-white facets of four diamonds, all of which had been sold to satisfy his creditors and assure her her college education. Like a racial memory, she'd often concluded, the impulse toward gems more often than not led her to the jewelers instead of the bank; while the checking account was always sufficient to cover her needs, her savings book was starving, her safe deposit box heavy.

As a result, the dealer knew her well, and often lent sincere and unmocking commiseration when she had to sell a diamond to pay a bill. It was a circle she traveled at least once a month.

"Mrs. Windsor, how good to see you again."

Natalie looked up from her musings and held out a hand to Helene Bradford, the wife and portly twin of the store's owner. "Mrs. Bradford, I need something to calm me down."

The grey-haired woman laughed dutifully, a ringless hand bouncing across her sagging breasts. "Well, dear, how about a necklace? I have just received some from Amsterdam . . ." and she wandered toward another case. Natalie refused to budge.

"No," she said. "A ring."

"What kind?" The question was more of a pounce, and Natalie wished she had the temper to play a game of fussing over diamonds and settings just to feed the gossip's fire. Sam, however, had effectively defused her.

"I'll just look a bit, Mrs. Bradford. You don't have to hang around. I know you're busy."

Mrs. Bradford stepped immediately out of her matron-servant role and glared at the otherwise empty shop. "Busy? Listen, when I get four people in here I feel like I should run out and hire some help. Busy! I should live so long."

Natalie poked gently at a velvet-lined tray in front of her. "Well, if you don't mind me saying so, you sure don't look like you're going out of business."

The laugh was closer to an irritated bark. "It's what they call local trade, Mrs. Windsor. The people from out of town I see in here wouldn't fill the park benches in a year."

"Is it really all that bad?"

The elder woman shrugged sadly, and Natalie's spending mood evaporated. She stalled for several minutes, then promised to return and buy out the inventory.

Mrs. Bradford didn't smile.

She walked, then, to the pocket park behind the library and sat on a redwood bench. She watched a squirrel cadge peanuts from three old men sitting opposite her. They clucked, whistled softly, and undermined the animal's natural fear until it was nipping the snacks directly from their unsteady fingers.

There was a breeze, and she shivered, pulled her coat tightly around her neck and reluctantly rose to return to work. A jay scolded her loudly and she looked up through the remaining leaves, and saw Adriana in her office window. There was a shifting spot of sun glare that made Natalie's eyes water, but it was obvious, nonetheless, that the Director was watching her.

Natalie waved, and slowly dropped her hand when the gesture was ignored.

Bloody snob, she thought. I hope a witch turns your scotch to milk.

Chapter 6

THE AFTERNOON, then, was a dreary repetition of the morning's tedium and Mrs. Hall's none-too-subtle interference into her life. Several times, the iron-haired woman made passing references to dalliances in the stacks and the library as a seraglio; and when Natalie was on the floor double-checking inventory or going through the Fine list with Miriam, she looked up to see the Director staring down at her from the gallery. "The crow's nest," the staff called the overhang, but she'd never before appreciated the double-edged meaning.

The day's saving grace was, as usual, Miriam. Just prior to four, she asked if it would be all right to take on the night shift duties. "I've got some studying to do for this stupid course in anthropology I got talked into, Nat," she explained, tugging nervously at her

119

hair. "I can close up and handle the late comers. Honest."

Surprisingly, her black eyes had brimmed moistly.

"You," Natalie said, "are a doll. I think if I stayed one more hour in this place I'd strangle the old bat."

Miriam grinned and leaned against the counter, waiting until a matron left with an armful of children's books. "I know what you mean," she said in a stage whisper. "Believe me, I do. Hey, by the way, did you have a good time Saturday night?"

The question came in a rush, and Natalie looked up sharply at the abrupt change of subject. There was a hesitant suspicion instantly dismissed; she'd almost succeeded in relegating the night to selective memory.

"Well, yes, as a matter of fact I did. It was interesting, to say the least. You sure looked like you were enjoying yourself." She tried a smile just this side of a leer and laughed aloud when the girl blushed.

"Mrs. Hall introduced us," Miriam said shyly. "He is Mr. Toal's nephew, I think. She said he needed some company his own age."

"Nice work if you can get it."

"Did you meet Mr. Toal?"

"Sort of." Indeed, she thought. "I think we communicate on different levels, though. Money versus poverty, that sort of thing."

Miriam nodded understanding. "I like your blouse," she said, reaching out to pull gently at the flowered collar. "You know, ever since you started messing around with that *Herald* guy, you get nakeder and nakeder."

Too astonished to say anything, she provoked a short laugh when she glanced down at herself. Her blouse was, in fact, open far enough to permit a provocative glimpse of winterpale skin, but . . . nakeder? No. Looser would be a better word. Her hands strayed to her hips; her slacks, however, did fit slightly more snugly, and her skirts were perhaps shorter than she ordinarily wore them. But why not? Was there a law that prohibited a little innocent flaunting in a library? Miriam, she decided, was imagining things.

The girl continued to tease her, snickering until Natalie relented in self-defense and let her believe a trap was being laid for the unsuspecting reporter.

The voice was a shroud from above them, "Ladies, isn't there enough work for you to do?"

They behaved, then, like guilty school girls, mumbling under the Director's stare, giggling when they escaped out of sight in the stacks. And when, ten minutes later, Mrs. Hall joined them to mutter about social improprieties and potentials for gossip, Natalie told her she was leaving early and the younger girl would be taking her place.

"Well, I don't know . . . might it not be better . . ."

"Mrs. Hall, I have a splitting headache, and there's nothing down here now that has to be done that Miriam can't do. Believe me, it's all right."

The Director made a pantomime of conflict, yielded and turned her shark's grin to Miriam as a gesture of trust none of them knew was genuine. Then she asked Natalie for the pass key. "Mine has been misplaced, dear," she said lamely. "I'll return it to you in the morning."

Furious, she yanked the key from its holder and nearly tossed it into Mrs. Hall's outstretched hand. Wisely, Miriam kept silent while Natalie retrieved her coat, said her good-bys and left.

Tomorrow, she promised as she stood outside the building. Tomorrow will be better. I'll tell Marc all about it, and he'll tell me what I did wrong and why I shouldn't be so angry and why there is no reason on earth why I shouldn't turn right around and put a fist into the old hag's nose.

A hand went automatically to button her coat, stalled, and dropped to her side. Oddly, the temperature seemed higher than it had been at lunchtime, and as she watched fog began to turn the night sky starless; there were no puffs of wind, no banks of grey rolling in from the empty fields—only a light mist settled. The street lamps became hazy with faint blue halos, and the edges of neon signs blurred as though seen under water. The traffic had reversed itself and, with several stores geared to a five-o'clock closing, the Pike momentarily engaged in a charade of a rush hour. The checker players had left, and the benches were deserted except for a boy and his girl, giggling, tickling, apparently reluctant to end the school day and separate.

"Jealous?"

She turned, a curse dying on her lips as the glass door hissed shut and Miriam made a mocking face before running back into the library's shadows. One of these days I'll kill that girl, she thought, and thrust back the vagrant accusation that the truth was beginning to hurt.

A step down, and she hesitated. The fog was thickening rapidly, having already erased the opposite side of the street and transformed the traffic into slow-motion cat-creatures prowling behind diffused torches. It was, suddenly, an unpleasant thought: to return home in the fog, and have only the light in the kitchen, the living room, the stairwell. The night's warmth took on a paradoxical chill. She thought of the graveyard.

Yanking at her collar, feeling beads of moisture weighing the fur down over her shoulders, she walked around the library to Centre Street and headed for the luncheonette. A plate of lasagna, a cup or two of espresso, and she would be able to face the dark street, and the hurricane fence.

The luncheonette was only at the next corner, but Natalie crossed the street before reaching it. A patrol car had sped past, drawing her eyes to Bradford's jewelry store. A connection was made, and curiosity made her act.

She stood under the mansard roof's overhang. The store was empty. When she entered, the warning chime sounded solemnly hollow. Several of the display cases were already covered in black velvet for the night, but now she had a purpose in her search, and she was impatient for Mrs. Bradford to pop out of her rabbit hole in the back. When she did, however, she was wearing a plastic raincoat and fussing with the folds of a collapsible hat.

"Mrs. Windsor!"

Natalie shrugged an apology. "I didn't know you were closing, Mrs. Bradford."

"I didn't either," she said, sourly, bustling around the case and, without appearing to be rude, herding her back toward the door, "but my husband called to remind me we have a dinner party to attend tonight. There are some customers one doesn't dare to ignore, I'm afraid."

"Oh, that's okay. I just wanted to ask you something."

Mrs. Bradford stopped her maneuvering and rummaged in her handbag. "Stupid keys," she muttered. "Well, go ahead, my dear, be my guest."

"My brother . . . rather, Chief Windsor. I was talking to him this afternoon, and he said . . . he said he bought a ring from you recently."

"He did?" She added a frown to her wrinkles, then shook her head.

"A gold ring?" Natalie prompted. "Two ruby chips with a silver inset between them? It's not a common design, I think."

"No," Mrs. Bradford said. "I'm sorry, Mrs. Windsor, but I really don't think the Chief purchased it from us. It sounds specially made, and we try not to handle accounts like that. They cost too much."

Natalie would have protested her lie further, but she found herself out on the sidewalk again, staring dumbly while the jeweler's wife extinguished the lights and set the alarms. She waved, then, at the woman's departing back, and recrossed the street to enter the luncheonette.

It was a five minute wait before she could get a booth to herself, not wanting to spend time on a stool at the counter, and another five before a harried waitress was able to take her order. Between times, she wondered how she'd managed to come up with such a lie, and why Mrs. Bradford's answer displeased her. There were, after all, half a dozen other stores along the street he could have been to.

Dumb, she told herself, and passed all thought into limbo while she ate and watched the customers slip in out of the fog, clean their plates, empty their cups, joke with the counterman and take their exits at the sound of the register. More hungry than she realized, she ordered a second helping of the overspiced pasta and, when she'd done, held the espresso cup to her lips and sipped as slowly as she could.

You're stalling, Natalie Windsor.

The luncheonette emptied. The fluorescent lights embedded in the ceiling took on a softer glow that reflected off the fog that had completely washed out the view from the store's long front window. Like characters in a shadow play, pedestrians slipped past with shoulders hunched and hats pulled low over faces. Couples huddled as though for warmth. Another patrol car ghosted by, identified only by its blue flashing lights.

You are stalling, Natalie Windsor.

She was sitting against the back wall, partially concealed by a rack of paperbacks running heavily to romances and Westerns. Occasionally, a customer would paw listlessly through them with scarcely a glance in her direction. Less frequently, the waitress would remember where she was and, without walking all the way back, raise an eyebrow, moving only when Natalie lifted an empty cup. Stalling, maybe, but enjoying the show, feeling the library and Mrs. Hall's accusations shatter to dust. She was feeling relaxed.

And anxious.

For Marc.

One more day, she thought, then blinked away a daydream when Simon Bains took a seat at the counter and ordered a slice of pie and a cup of coffee. The waitress, poking suddenly at her unkempt hair and pulling at her apron, was obviously surprised to see the banker so long after hours. Her lips moved, and though Natalie could not hear the question, the answer was clear enough. Bains was angry, and disgusted.

"Directors' meeting tonight," he snapped, and drank his coffee as though it were a double shot of scotch. He reached into his raincoat and pulled out a handkerchief to dab at his lips. "It's a lousy business, you know. You work late when you don't want to, and it's too blasted late to go home for a decent meal without you having to rush to get back. So here I have to stay. Blast! You ever have a Directors' meeting?"

Again the waitress's voice was too low to hear, and Bains's added comment was muffled by the action of the handkerchief.

Natalie surveyed the imported coat, the handmade shoes, the careful lay of Bains's long black hair. She shook her head. You live a hard life, Simon old crock, she thought.

She was considering calling out a greeting when, pursuing his anger, Bains dipped into his trouser pocket to scoop out a fistful of change which he slapped on the counter. There was a space of several seconds, then, when the tableau froze: the waitress quickly totaling the money with her eyes; Bains in the act of rising; Natalie staring at his hand; the light catching and starring the ruby chips on the ring he was wearing.

*   *   *

A single peculiar ring was not to be questioned. It was. It existed. In the shoe box in the den. Two, and because it was Sam's, was odd but not worrisome. Three, however, transformed that oddity into the commonplace, and there was nothing common about the design of that ring.

Reluctantly, she shuffled through memories, searching for the first time she'd seen Ben's ring. The moment eluded her, more as she searched and finally she told herself to let it go, that it would come eventually.

And as she paid her bill and buttoned her coat, it did.

Ben had been part of an escort at some forgotten merchant's funeral. Supposedly, it had been his day off, one of two before he moved to the night shift, and he'd spent most of the morning polishing his brass and turning his boots into blackly embossed mirrors. A call had come—and he'd dashed out into the rain. When he returned, he was wearing the ring, sheepishly admitting he'd hoped it would add something to his image. She'd teased him so much he'd only worn it a couple of times afterward. At least, she'd always believed it was a result of her teasing.

She stepped into the fog, blinking at the dampness, frowning at the temperature that had twisted back on itself again.

The collar pushed into her face as she walked. There was still a light in the library, and she was tempted to drop in on Miriam to help her pass the time. Tempted, but only that, and she quickened her steps toward home. If it hadn't been for Bains, she would have succumbed, but she knew the girl's bright chatter would have only aggravated an irrational disquiet. A truck startled her by blaring through the fog, and she was briefly reminded of a locomotive barreling through midnight across an open field, blasting its horn at a crossing deserted by everything except the stars.

At Fox Road she paused before attempting to cross the Pike. She felt as though she were floating. The bulbs of the street lights were disembodied. Her breathing was amplified. Water dripped slowly into the gutter from an invisible tree.

She was halfway over when she froze.

A grumbling. Pitched too high to be a truck, not high enough for an automobile. In the road's dark island center the fog was a clammy dusting on her cheeks, but thick enough to prevent headlights' penetration. She ran, sensed the curb and slowed, nearly stumbling when her shoes slid in the gutter.

Suddenly, she was blinded. Headlights exploded. She threw an arm over her eyes, whipped it down when she realized the vehicle was swerving. She had time enough to think *a drunk!* before uttering a short gasping scream. She spun blindly on the sidewalk, as the headlights pulled the grumbling behind them, bounced when they struck the curb and canted wildly as the vehicle raced toward the center of town. There were no taillights.

"I don't believe it," she said, stepped back and stumbled into a hedge. "I don't believe it."

She trembled and, heedless of the pricks the shrub inflicted on her palms, grabbed at the hedge to steady herself. The single light between the corner and her house winked once, and she pushed away, afraid to run and too shaken to walk at a normal pace.

"He had to be drunk," she said aloud, needing the sound to smother the sharp crack of her heels on the sidewalk. "Nobody runs that fast on a night like this. Nobody! Stupid drunk ought to be locked up." She laughed when she remembered her demand that the police leave her alone; where were they when she needed them? "What an idiot!" and she wasn't sure whether she was talking about herself or the driver.

By the time she reached the house, her teeth had stopped their chattering, her stomach finally suppressed the lurching that carried a hint of acid to her mouth. With one hand tight to her chest she climbed the porch steps and pulled her purse in front of her to hunt for her keys.

"How do I get so much junk . . ."

Her fingers touched metal, lost it, and she cursed loudly and turned to glare at the invisible street. The street light winked again, and went out. There was nothing left: the fog covered it all from the Pike to the fence, and for the first time in months she felt herself wishing for neighbors, anyone to have a light on in one of the other five houses on the block.

She shifted her weight as her hands dipped into the purse again, and the floorboard beneath her creaked loudly, seemed to echo. She sighed in relief when the key ring slipped over her finger, smiled to herself as she tested each key, hoping to find by feel alone the one she needed so she wouldn't have to run through them all before escaping inside.

"Come on," she muttered impatiently. "Come on, you stupid little . . ." She scraped one key after another over the lock, trying to remember where she'd accumulated so many, and why. "Come on!"

Her face was doubly moist now, perspiration adding its stickiness to the fog's residue. She wiped a sleeve roughly over her lips, her brow, and bent to try one more time.

Then she hesitated, and looked back over her shoulder.

There was something moving in the grass. Lightly, too light for a footfall. An animal. Without knowing why, she covered the key with her fingers, easing it slowly into place, feeling each serration slide into its position. The animal—cat? dog? her imagination refused to speculate further—brushed by the forsythia at the base of the porch. Moving cautiously, not merely wandering.

For no reason at all, Natalie knew it was stalking.

When she heard the padding reach the bottom step, she jammed the key home, wrenching it over and shoved open the door, throwing herself inside and slamming it closed behind her. She cried out, then, when a heavy weight thumped against the outside, as though something had been thrown after her.

The house was cold.

She felt the flagstones' dampness seep through her shoes as she backed slowly away from the door. With lights neither inside nor out, she could see no shadows through the frosted glass, but whatever had leaped after her was large enough to cause the porch to protest under its back and forth pacing. It made no attempts to be silent. As though it sensed she was alone. Another thump against the thick wood, and she backed another step toward the stairwell. Her purse dropped to the floor, and the jarring clatter of keys seemed to alert the thing on the porch. It threw itself a third time against the house, followed with a frenzied scratching at the base of the door.

And as suddenly as it arrived, it was gone.

Natalie listened, heard nothing but the sound of her own breath's rasping. Slowly, she moved forward and pressed against the door, tried to wipe some clarity into the glass, but could see nothing but black.

A conflict, then: her eyes demanded light, and her nerves as well, but her hands refused to move toward a switch. A light would admit to whatever had chased her that she was still inside. A light would throw shadows.

But it was cold, and she needed some warmth.

Scratching. She whirled around. The back door—surely it was locked. It was always locked.

The french doors at the head of the stairs. The scratching thundered around the stairwell, converged and deafened her. She stumbled forward, shedding her coat unconsciously, crawling on hands and knees to the second floor. And as she tested the lock and found it engaged, she heard a scrabbling on the deck and muffled a scream with her hands. Beyond the white curtains, through the clear glass, there was night. And a darker shape. She knew it was impossible for her to be seeing it. There was no moon, no stars, and the fog had blanketed the street lights. Yet it was there, unmistakably: a shadow cast against the air. The texture of the curtains prevented her from distinguishing size and shape accurately; sensations, only, of a feline creature whose eyes would have reflected crimson if there'd been any light.

It did nothing. Waited. Crouched.

Still braced on knees and palms, Natalie felt her elbows begin to tremble. She wanted to ease back onto her heels, but a move would betray her and the doors were glass.

Wait, she ordered, and stared at the darkness until lights began to swirl across her vision in brilliant gold nebulae. She lowered her lids, held them tight to a count of ten. The spinning vanished, but in its place a throbbing that worked like a tide from the base of her neck to the top of her skull. Her hair became weighted, and a draft from the storage room to her right wafted vagrant strands against her cheeks, her nose, tickled at her lips. She locked her elbows to still the quivering and felt the perspiration on her palms, the sudden stiffness of the carpeting stinging her skin.

Crouched. Waiting. A jungle cat, she thought, deciding if it was hungry.

Hold it, Sam! I think I saw something ... I just got a glimpse ... it ... cat ... big thing ... it looks ...

The house became vocal, the night noises she'd taken for granted billowing until they screamed.

The furnace clicking on in the basement, a muffled roaring that vibrated through the floors; the refrigerator whining shrilly to drown the maddeningly steady buzzing of the kitchen clock; the notch by notch clicking of the bedroom's clock radio; the age of the house itself groaning under the weight of the fog—the roof shifting, porches pulling into themselves, the crinoline rustling of curtains, paper crackling of shades.

And through it all, all of it making her duck her head into her chest, a ringing.

My God, she thought suddenly, I've moved!

She raised her head and looked toward the doors. The creature, the presence, had vanished, and there was nothing now but unrelieved blackness.

And the ringing of the telephone.

Her first inclination was to collapse, to draw knees and elbows into her chest and huddle against the malevolence that continued to infect the atmosphere. But the telephone was strident, unrelenting; whoever it was wouldn't surrender until she answered.

Cramps threatened to tear at her legs as she pushed herself to her feet and stumbled blindly around the bannister into the bedroom, snatching at the air until her hands met the receiver on her night table. The instrument fell, bounced on the floor, and she could hear the tinny sound of a voice querulously demanding. Slumping to her knees, she pressed the cold plastic to her ear.

"Nattie, is that you? Nattie, do you hear me? Are you all right, Nattie? Nattie, can you hear me?"

Elaine's voice was curiously flat, the questions almost perfunctory.

"My God, Elaine, thank God it's you."

There was a silence, prolonged until Natalie

wondered if she'd been hearing things. But there was no dial tone.

"Elaine? Elaine, that is you, isn't it?"

"Nattie, Nattie, why didn't you answer the telephone? Were you in the shower or something? Are you all right?"

Natalie hesitated only a moment. "I'm fine, Elaine. I'm sorry, but yes, I was in the shower."

"But why were you . . . I mean, it sounds like you're crying or something. Are you sure you're all right?"

"Yes," she said firmly. "I'm fine. I was daydreaming and the phone startled me. I think," and she laughed weakly, "I scared myself. It's that kind of night."

Another silence, and she couldn't understand why the woman was behaving so oddly. And she's not, she told herself instantly; it's you, idiot. You're not hearing straight after . . . after . . .

"It is that kind of night," Elaine said finally. "That's why I called. I thought maybe you'd like some company. Sam said there isn't anything moving anywhere, and he was worried about you. He thought maybe you'd like to come over to see us for a while. Watch some television or something, okay?"

It was too much. After all that happened already, what she definitely did not need now was Elaine's mockery of pity spilling into her house. She was right to lie; if she'd explained what had happened, they'd begin again the nonsense about the psychiatrist.

"No," she said when the offer was repeated. "No, it's okay, Elaine. I was reading some book in the library today, one of those Gothic things, and the fog just touched on my overdrive imagination."

"Well, if you're sure . . ."

"I'm sure, but thanks for calling. It's nice to know someone's out there, if you know what I mean."

"Oh, I do, Nattie, I do. Well . . . if you're sure, dear, then I'd better ring off. Sam will be home soon, and you know how he is if there isn't a snack waiting for him as soon as he walks in the door." She laughed shrilly, in staccato bursts. "Biggest eater in the country, I swear to heaven."

Natalie agreed, but was reluctant to let Elaine hang up. She asked, then, about her day and immediately tuned out the response while she eased onto the bed and switched on the light. The room grew, the bulb under the white shade seemed more fire than filament, and for the first time since she'd left the luncheonette, she felt her lungs working normally.

"Where is Sam?" she asked suddenly, unaware that she was interrupting.

"Oh, out," Elaine said. "You know how men are, dear. They decide to meet with the boys and run a few hands of poker or whatever it is they play when we girls aren't around." She laughed again, and Natalie held the receiver away from her ear until it died down. "Ben, the poor dear, he never won anything according to Sam. Could never concentrate, Sam says."

"Sam does a lot of talking."

"What was that?"

"Just a joke, Elaine. Well, look, I don't want you to get into trouble on my account. You get Sam's snacks together and maybe I'll call you tomorrow."

"All right, Nattie. Are you sure you're all right, now?"

"Sure. Right as rain. Thanks for calling, Elaine."

When the voice clicked into a dial tone, she replaced the receiver and hugged herself. The menace, she was positive, was gone, but she sat on the bed for nearly an hour before fetching a cardigan from the closet and returning downstairs. She picked up her coat, dusted it off and folded it over a chair in the living room. Then, methodically, she turned on all the lights in the house.

It was gone, she reminded herself, but the glow would keep out the fog while she gave herself a chance to think. And in thinking, wandered, touching furniture, paneling, pictures on the walls until she found herself standing in the silence of the den.

The shoe box was still on the table where she and Marc had left it.

Staring. Doubts that resolved themselves into a belief of a definite connection among the men wearing Ben's ring. Carefully, she lifted the lid, pushed aside the mementos most of which she could no longer place, and extracted the gold band.

How extraordinarily ordinary, she thought as she held it under the desk lamp. No inscriptions, no markings of any kind except for the gems and the silver. It wasn't even handsome. Not handsome, or smart, or even fashionable, especially for a small-town policeman. Was it really possible that he and Sam and banker Bains were members of some secret men's club? She grinned absently; who the hell knows? She'd never found it easy to understand the complexity that made men as labyrinthian as they claimed women to be.

She sat in the armchair and placed the ring on her fingers, smiled at the size, even bigger than her thumb. She tossed it into the air, caught it and tossed again. She stared at the empty bookcases, narrowing her eyes in an attempt to bring into focus something that nagged at the fringes of her vision.

Then she shook her head and closed a fist over the ring. Out of sight and all that, she thought, and shifted her puzzlement to the stalking creature.

A combination of fog and reaction to the drunken driver had in all probability sensitized her imagination until she'd created an actual menace.

She held that thought as she replaced the ring, closed up the den and went into the kitchen for a cup of tea.

A glance at the clock. It was already past nine.

"Confound it, Natalie, you've wasted the whole evening being chased by ghosts."

The next day Marc would be back from the city. She would tell him everything and feel like a small girl frightened by a grandmother's Halloween story as he carefully, thoughtfully, explained to her what she'd already known.

The next day.

Marc.

The telephone rang.

And when she answered it, heard the voice, heard the message, she slumped to the floor in a whirlpool of black.

Chapter 7

*T*HE BED was her own. The quilt was tucked lightly against her sides, the pillow stiffly cool with a fresh sheath of linen. Without opening her eyes, she sensed company in the room, but kept her head still until it stopped playing at carousel. And when it did, seconds later, she gasped at the memory of the call.

"Natalie?"

Quietly, as in a hospital, overlaid with fear and a concern rooted deeper than worry. Hands pressed her shoulders, and she felt the bed give beneath her. A kiss fluttered against her cheek.

And still, her eyes remained closed.

Natalie?

Yes, is that you Sam? I was just talking to Elaine.

Natalie, I thought you were working tonight.

I was going to, but Adriana gave me a pain in the neck, as well as in other portions of my undernourished anatomy. I begged off the late hours and Miriam Burke volunteered to take my place. She said she had some studying. She's taking a college course, you know.

I thought you were working late.

I just told you, Sam.

Well, you're damned lucky, Natalie.

Sam, such language! I thought—what do you mean, I'm lucky? What's wrong, Sam? What's happened?

There was a light on in the library after hours. One of my men stopped by, thinking maybe it was you spending our money again. The door was smashed open.

Oh, God, Sam!

There was glass all over the place. He found Miriam behind the front desk.

Oh, my God.

All cut up, she was.

Oh, Sam, the poor little—

It could have been you, Natalie. You were supposed to be there tonight, not her.

The voice was loud, clear, as though she were listening to a tape recorder.

It could have been you, Natalie. You were supposed to be there tonight, not her.

"Nat, are you okay?

She opened her eyes and turned her head. A chair from the other bedroom had been placed by her side. A figure made dark by the position of the lamp leaned toward her and she cringed until she saw the hand on her shoulder. Then she sat up and reached out her arms.

Marc held her, then, and rocked slowly, crooning wordlessly into her ear, stroking her hair and pulling it back from her face. He stroked her cheek, her neck, drew the hand back and it brushed over the tip of her breast. She shuddered and sought a resting place on his chest. She licked her lips and tasted encrusted salt. Unconscious but crying, and the skin was stiff between eyes and chin.

"Nat?"

He eased her away but didn't release her arms.

"Miriam," she said, and he dropped a finger to her lips, sealing them. Then he looked over the bed, and she turned to see Elaine hovering by the bureau, fussing with the toiletries scattered haphazardly on the top. When she saw Natalie staring at her, she drew her hands primly to her stomach and the look of disapproval was too plain to be ignored, too comical to let pass without a laugh.

"Hysterical," Elaine said. "I told you we should have gotten a doctor."

"Nonsense," Marc said, equally annoyed. "All she needs is some rest. After what you told me about tonight, it's small wonder she fainted. News like that isn't the easiest in the world to take without some warning, you know."

They spoke in whispers, arguing, and Natalie realized they were maneuvering for territorial rights; and it was pleasant for a while listening to Marc establishing his claim without asking for her support. But the sniping and whining became tedious, and she stopped it with a fresh outburst of crying that ceased only when Elaine left to fetch her a glass of water.

Marc sat back, then, leaving one hand to grip both of hers. He looked tired, blue-black pouches under his eyes complemented unkindly the sag of his shoulders, the unkempt thatch of his hair.

"You gave me a start, librarian," he said.

"Oh, my God, Marc, what am I going to do?"

He frowned, but she forestalled an explanation when Elaine returned with the water. Grateful for the cool liquid, she drained the glass and asked for another, grinning at the she-needs-me-not-you glare Elaine shot at Marc as she left.

"Can you stay?" she whispered.

"As you want," he said unhesitatingly. "But what about her?"

Natalie coughed over another spasm of laughter. "Don't let it bother you. She'll love every dirty minute of it."

"Are you promising something, or what?"

"Or what," she said, and allowed him to ease her back onto her pillow. Elaine returned and was miffed when the offered glass was refused.

"I still think a doctor—"

"No, Elaine," she said wearily. "I just want to rest a minute."

She scowled and took a position on the other side of the bed, straightening the quilt and turning back its satin edge neatly. "I'll wait up until you fall asleep. I'm sure Mr. Clayton has to go to work in the morning."

"Who, me?" Marc shook a cigarette from a battered pack and lighted it. "My boss thinks I've done enough work for one week." He looked at Elaine and smiled innocently. "I have the rest of the time off. Been to the city, you know. Big doings down there."

"I can imagine," Elaine sniffed. "Well, perhaps I can get us a cup of coffee."

"No, thanks," Natalie said. "I'm really not in the mood. Why don't you get back to Sam? He must be tired from his night out."

"Night out?" Elaine seemed puzzled, then widened her eyes. "Oh, yes, that. No, not really. Just a friendly card game, I told you. I have all the time in the world. What with this . . . thing interrupting him, I don't know when he'll be back. And really, Nattie, you shouldn't be staying up so late. Not if you expect to go to work tomorrow."

Natalie was spared a comment when the phone rang and Elaine rushed to grab it from the nightstand. Then she placed a hand over the receiver. "It's Sam." Natalie shook her head.

"She can't talk to you now, Sammy. No, she's fine. Just a shock to hear about poor little Miriam. No, she can't talk to you now. Can't it wait until morning? Why don't you go out and hunt up some clues or something? Yes, I'll be here for a while. No. No. Well, if you insist, Sam, I'm sure she'll be all right. Mr. Clayton is here with her. That's right, the reporter. I know, Sam, I know. I'll be right home. Right away."

She hung up and turned to Natalie, pointedly ignoring Marc's raised eyebrows. "That was Sam. He says he needs me home for something." She plumped at her sagging chest and reached for the coat thrown at the foot of the bed. "I'm glad I could help, Nattie dear. I'll call you tomorrow to see how you're doing. Maybe you should take time off until you recover. When was the last time you had a vacation, anyway?"

"Thanks, Elaine," Natalie said, her voice acting as hands to push her toward the door. "I appreciate your coming over. I'll call you, okay? And tell Sam . . ." She shook her head. "Never mind. I'll be in touch, okay?"

It was clearly not all right, but Elaine had

apparently been given her orders over the phone, and she huffed out with as much dignity as remained to her. The house was silent until the front door slammed.

Immediately, Natalie threw back the quilt and sat up. Marc stared, and she was confused until she looked down and saw her blouse opened to the waist. Flustered, then irked at his schoolboy leer, she stood and worked at the buttons.

"What's the matter? You never saw a woman undressed before?"

"Depends on the woman you want to see undressed," he said, rising and following her out of the room and around to the french doors. "Now suppose you tell me what you meant by the cat on the roof?"

Natalie turned with one hand on the bannister. "When did I say that?"

"While you were unconscious. Come on, Nat, something else happened here besides the news about Miriam. What was it?"

"Why are you home?" she countered. "You weren't supposed to be back until tomorrow."

"You answer my question, I'll answer yours."

"No," she said, feigning a pout and sitting on the top step. "You first, me second. I have a feeling mine is going to take quite a bit longer."

He'd been, he said, thoroughly bored with the entire week. All he'd done was sit in on charcoal pinstripes bantering and baiting about the state of the economy. Toal was present in his capacity as a multimillionaire with various important investments world-wide. But what the entire series of meetings boiled down to was a general gripe session, a demand for a change of administration in Washington, and a wondering aloud how Toal managed to keep his calm and his head above water; the Oxrun representative was apparently an exception to a financial rule.

"He's a duck, I can tell you," said Marc. "Never said a word the entire time I sat in—purely as an observer, you understand. He just nodded when someone looked at him, frowned when everyone else did, and acted as though he was the most bored man on earth, next to me. For the life of me, I can't understand why Dederson wanted me down there. What a bloody waste it was!"

"So you came back."

He smiled crookedly. "I came back. Decided to pay you a visit and found Elaine at the door. And then we found you."

"Nice of you to come."

"I almost didn't. Drove past the Station three times in fact, the fog was so thick. And you know something? When I finally made the right turn, I remembered I had trouble like that twice before, after Toal's party. Curious." He waved away the observation with an abortive try at a smoke ring. "Must be Freudian. I don't like it here, my mind tells me to miss the turn-offs, and when my id reminds me I can't go anywhere else the way the economy is, I suddenly find the way in. Psychology One. Amherst. Brilliant student, I might add."

Natalie rested her chin on her palm, her elbow braced on a knee. Elaine had turned off the lights downstairs, and only the bulb over their heads illuminated the foyer.

"I guess I played the cavalier tonight, didn't I?" he added softly.

She assured him he did and, after shifting to lie on her back and stare at the ceiling, she told him everything she could remember of the day.

"And it's odd, because Sam was wrong. I wasn't supposed to be at the library tonight. I cleared it with Mrs. Hall at least an hour before the day shift ended. At least an hour."

"Noted," he said, and stretched out beside her. He let a hand settle onto her stomach, hesitated until it was apparent she wasn't going to move it. Then he began a circling motion that made her feel at once tense and loose. Muscles rippled under his touch, and there was a curious aching in her breasts and thighs. She told herself she didn't need sign posts to show her where she was heading, but neither, oddly, did she want to go there just yet. Not tonight. At least, not now.

"Marc," and her hand rested atop his. "Marc, I want to look outside."

"For the cat-thing, or whatever? I don't blame you," he said, snapping to his feet and pulling her after him. "But first, there's a little matter of some temptation," and before she could stop him, he reached over and fastened the center button, one she'd forgotten. Then his face clouded sorrowfully. "A hundred years from now I'll never believe I did that."

The fog had not lifted, but the temperature had returned to October normal. They started at the back, Marc carrying a flashlight whose broad beam easily turned the eleven o'clock darkness into a semblance of dusk. But there was nothing they could see that served as evidence of a climbing. Moisture clung to the pillars under the deck in beaded clusters, and though they nearly touched noses to the wood, they found no scratch marks, no scrapes. Around the side of the house, then, inches at a time while the white light swept carefully over the fog-laden grass. Again there was nothing, either on the lawn or alongside the house where grass gave way to bare earth around the shrubs. By the time they arrived back at the front door, Natalie was ready to scream, so positive had she become that her mind had not been playing her tricks.

On the porch, she shook her collar and squealed when moisture whipped across her face and down her neck. Then she knelt and directed the light at the front door.

"Nothing."

Marc moved beside her. "You're right again, lady. Nothing at all."

He took her elbow, waiting until she decided the direction: to the railing, where she stood watching as the flashlight beam was devoured by the fog. "It's cold," he said, but she ignored him and he settled by leaning against the post. A moment later, the street light blinked on, an instant rising of a blue-white sun curtained by a thin, shifting cloud.

A dog barked several blocks away; a patrol car wailed down the Pike toward Mainland Road. The fog seemed to sigh as though wearying of carrying its own load, and it began to drizzle. The houses across the street reflected the street light in shades of grey against gleaming black.

Finally, she swallowed and tucked the collar closer to her chin.

"I know it now, Marc. I know it as sure as we're standing here, and I don't know why."

A match flared, creating shadows on his face, then dimmed to a pulsing orange ember that traced golden arcs from mouth to side to mouth again.

"I've been trying to reason out all that's happened, thinking there really can't be a connection between me and what's going on with the others. I even convinced myself that I was drunk that night in the library. But I wasn't, Marc. I wasn't drunk. You've seen me drink more than I had then. Was I drunk? Was I?"

There was, gratefully, no answer.

"Marc, either someone's trying to drive me nuts—to drive me into a padded cell for the rest of my life—or someone's trying to kill me. I know it, but I can't prove it, that that truck deliberately tried to run me down; I know, even though you saw there were no tracks, that something was out here tonight trying to break into the house, to tear me apart like . . . Ben . . . like Vorhees."

"And Miriam," he said, without commitment.

"And Miriam. Oh, my God, poor Miriam! All she wanted to do was study for some stupid course of hers. She wanted to be a university librarian, you know, so she could meet a professor and go to teas and fight politics with the other wives. Can you imagine it? Fighting politics with the other wives." She gulped air, exhaled slowly and saw puffs of white spinning into the rain; the fog had lifted. "I was supposed to be there tonight. I was supposed to be the one that got it, Marc. Ever since I started fooling around with that computer list, Adriana has been on my back. Remember when I told you I wouldn't be surprised if our computer time was taken from us? Well, it was. And Miriam . . ."

The cigarette rocketed into the yard, winked out instantly as it struck the grass. Another match, another orange ember.

"All right," she said, "tell me I'm developing all the classic symptoms of paranoia. Tell me there's nothing out there waiting for you to go home, nothing in the library that would make someone want to kill me. For God's sake, Marc, tell me!"

She waited, biting at her lower lip, not

fighting tears but an incomprehensible urge to explode into laughter. All her careful reasonings, all the rationalizations, gone in a five-minute talk with a man in a shadow. Maybe Sam and Elaine had been right all along; maybe she was pushing herself into insanity.

Insanity.

It was, in some ways, a comforting thought.

Marc lit a third cigarette.

"Well?" she said.

"You remember that first night a million years ago when I wanted to talk to you at the party, and somehow we never got the chance?"

She nodded, thinking: the miracles were gone, only mazes left.

"Well, I was having trouble with Dederson, see. Not the tripe story kind I always grouse about, but something I think is more serious. I wasn't here, see, when you moved into town. I came a few months later. It's a hard place to get to know. So few people, so few doors that will open to you even if you are a member of the Fourth Estate. Anyway, I spent most of my time rewriting until the old man decided I was competent enough to handle a few articles on my own. That's why I missed the story of your husband's murder." He pushed off the post and stood beside it, turning his back on the street to stare at the living room windows. "When Vorhees was killed, I tried interviewing Sam Windsor and the officer who discovered the body. I wasn't surprised when no one wanted to talk. An embarrassment and all that. Small towns aren't supposed to breed the symptoms of grisly big-city killings. Unfortunately, Dederson wouldn't even let me run the story from the fact sheet the police eventually handed out. He killed it."

"Did you talk to him? Maybe there was a reason."

"I talked and he listened and then he told me, plain and simple: no story, no panic. Like no one would ever hear of it if it wasn't in his precious paper."

"I'm sorry, Marc, but I don't understand. What does all this have—"

"Nat, are you tired?"

She laughed once, and shrugged. "No, I guess not."

"I mean, could you stand to walk a little with me?"

"In the rain?"

He grinned, and without thinking, she reached out and traced a finger over his lips. He took her hand, kissed it and released her. "In the rain," he said. "It's cold and miserable and I think I love you and I want to tell you a few things while we walk. Let's call it a direct experience experiment."

"Umbrella?"

"No," and he took her arm to lead her down the steps. "Let's get soaked and pray for pneumonia to give us a few days off."

They walked silently to the corner, turned toward Mainland Road. The drizzle had eased, and the cool mask falling on her face felt less discomforting than soothing. It was easy for her to believe at that moment that she and Marc were the only ones left in the world.

"I don't like not being able to write," he said suddenly as they passed the darkened church. "And it seemed awfully unprofessional to kill a story that would have surely sold more papers. Like it or not, gore is what brings in the loot. Messy, but true. So I bugged Windsor some more, and got myself politely but firmly tossed out on my ear. I spent a lot of time walking around. I went for drives to no place in particular. That's when I kept getting lost. Which, on the face of it, is ridiculous. How anyone can get lost around here is beyond me. But I did it."

"The party," she said. "Was it punishment for not letting go?"

He nodded. "I'm sure of it. And what Toal said to me that night about the statue could have been sent to the paper on a three-by-five card. Dederson gave it a four-column headline with a six-column picture. There was nothing about our adventure in the library. No comments from anyone about Vorhees' death. Nothing. Not even a statement of what a tragedy it was for the college. Not a thing."

"But—"

"Wait. Don't talk. Just walk."

At the end of the Pike, he turned her around and pointed back toward the town's center. "No traffic, right?"

"Sure, but for crying out loud, it's close to midnight on a week night. Who in heaven's name is going to be cruising around here?"

"Nobody," he said. "And if you think about it, no one does during daylight either."

"What?" But he said nothing, forcing her to conjure as typical a day as she could, then suddenly remembering a notion that had come to her less than a week ago: that all the traffic seemed to flow out of the Station in the morning, back again at night. And Mrs. Bradford, complaining that most of her customers were locals, and the out-of-towners who did stop seldom returned.

"Okay?" he said.

"I don't know. I guess so."

"Okay. Now follow me." He turned around and, after a bus had sprayed past them, he ran to the opposite side of the highway, dragging her with him.

"Now," he said, "take a good long look at what you see."

She followed his pointing finger, first to the traffic light, then in a slow sweep from right to left. Mercury arc lamps were evenly spaced along the cross-state road, certainly bright enough to illuminate the shoulders for several yards around them. Yet, and she had to strain to see, the shoulders directly opposite were just as well lighted, and harder to see clearly.

"Optical illusion," she said. "A trick of the rain and the traffic and the night."

"Okay," he said, pulling her farther along

the road. "Now I'll show you something else."

"I wish you'd tell me," she said.

"No. I don't want you to . . ." and they'd gone perhaps two hundred yards before he about-faced and began walking back. "You stay behind me about ten paces or so, and tell me when I'm exactly opposite the Pike. Exactly, Nat, you understand?"

She didn't, really, but did as she was bidden. Then, "Hold it, Deerslayer!" She ran up to him and stared into his eyes. "So? Here we are."

"Good for you," he said, his voice hinting at a quaver. "If you hadn't told me, Nat, I would have walked right past it. You'll have to believe me when I tell you that when I look across the street, all I can see are trees. No Pike. No light. No corner houses. I couldn't even pick out my office from here."

"You're kidding."

"Nat, you think someone is trying to kill you or maybe drive you nuts for some reason. I believe it. Now you have to believe me when I say someone is trying to keep me out of this town."

Chapter 8

THURSDAY WAS silent as Natalie reluctantly kissed Marc good-by at the corner and watched him walk away toward his office. He'd stayed the night, sleeping in the spare room, had awakened her with a bachelor's breakfast overcooked and undernourishing. Neither felt much like talking about the evening before. The only words passed in glances, not quite accidental touches of hands, and the careful way she held his coat for him at the front door.

The library was in mourning. Adriana had not come in except for a brief hour before eleven to tell the staff they'd be given half a day in honor of Miriam's passing. Nobody worked, and Natalie's mood wasn't helped at all by Arlene's constant sniffling. By one, she'd had enough and ran to the grocer's to fetch dinner for two, giving her a giddily pleasant feeling that lasted until she arrived back home in time to catch the telephone's shrill command.

It was Sam, requesting she drop by the station some time that afternoon.

"An inquiry, Sam?"

"I'm afraid so, Nat."

She agreed to come immediately, made a quick call to the newspaper and was told Marc was out on assignment.

Lovely, she thought as she dashed back out again. Probably some idiot flower show, or whatever it is women's clubs have two days before Halloween.

And as she crossed the Pike, she stopped suddenly and looked to her right. There were no cars moving in her direction. And to her left, only a slow drifting in and out of the side streets where the shops were located.

It was the same on High Street and Steuben Avenue, both of which emptied onto the Mainland Road.

When she reached Chancellor and turned to walk up to the police station, she was trembling in spite of the Indian summer heat that had again driven off the clouds and replaced them with a startling blue. She told herself the lack of traffic was only the time of day, but she didn't quite believe it.

"Hey, Mrs. Windsor!"

Just outside headquarters she stopped and turned around. A young boy was running toward her, and it was a confusing moment before she recognized a teen-ager who practically lived in the library's astronomy section.

As he loped to a halt, she struggled to fit a name to the thin and bespectacled face. "Andy!" she said, holding out a hand and trying not to wince as he squeezed it. "What can I do for you?"

"Mrs. Windsor, I . . . I'm sorry about Miss Burke."

And the day took on the shroud she'd almost managed to shed.

"But I had this book of hers, see, and I was going to return it this afternoon, but I went to the library and it was closed."

He looked as though he was going to cry.

"Don't worry about it, Andy. Tomorrow'll do just fine."

"No," he said, shaking his head violently. "No, you see, we're moving this afternoon. I really don't have the money to pay for it, and I didn't want you to think I'd steal from you because I wouldn't. I never have, you know."

"Hey," she said, suppressing a smile. "There's no problem, no problem at all. You just wait until you're settled in your new house and then drop it in the mail. I'll make sure we don't send the Gestapo charging after you."

He brightened and shook her hand vigorously. "Hey, now that's cool, Mrs. Windsor, really. No kidding, thanks a lot. Really. Hey, I got to go. I'm really sorry about . . . well, you know. See you around, Mrs. Windsor, and thanks a lot."

A whirlwind, and he was gone, leaving her

breathless. Another one gone, she thought as she climbed the short flight of steps to the station. There had been so many over the past year, she didn't know how the town managed to stay on its feet when, by all rights, it should have been long on the road to dying.

Sam was waiting at the office door, officially solemn, almost pompously so. He led her quickly inside, introduced her to the police stenographer and apologized for the occasion. She nodded, and gripped her hands in her lap.

"Natalie," he began after seating himself behind his desk and lifting a manila folder in the cradle of his hands, "you knew Miriam Burke, is that right?"

"You know it is, Sam."

"Natalie, please." He pointed to the stenographer. "This poor guy has to take down every word you say. Have a heart and play the game, okay?"

She shrugged. "If it'll make you feel better, Sam."

"Okay. So you knew Miriam Burke. Does she usually work late nights?"

"No, I do. The late hours were my idea, you know, and I usually volunteered for them."

"Then why did Miriam work late last night?"

"I had a headache, and she wanted someplace quiet to study. She asked if she could switch with me and I said sure, why not? Adriana okayed it."

"Mrs. Hall?"

"Right."

"So except for Mrs. Hall, everyone else had a right to expect you to be working there last night."

"Sure," and she couldn't contain herself: "Sam, are you trying to say that whoever did . . . that thing to Miriam—"

He waved a massive hand and she quieted. "I am saying nothing, Natalie. I just want to be clear on what happened. Where, exactly, were you last night?"

"Home," she said, flatly. "Alone."

"I'm sure you were."

"At least until I got your call about Miriam. Then Marc and Elaine came over." She looked straight at him and admired the control he exhibited when she added, "Elaine left early. Marc stayed around a while after."

"You, uh, had no trouble while you were home?"

"No, should I have?" She asked the question quickly, without thinking, and was startled to see his eyes narrow. Don't, she ordered herself then, don't interpret, just observe.

"Nonsense, I was just looking for . . . forget it. So you went home with this headache and . . ."

"And puttered around until I got the call, and I fainted, and Marc and Elaine were there and that's all, Chief."

"You're right about that," he said stiffly. "That's all. All right, Kevin," he said to the stenographer, "you type that up and bring it back for Mrs. Windsor to sign. You can stay awhile, can't you?"

"Sure," she said. "Adriana closed the library. I'm just killing time until Marc gets back from an assignment."

"Oh, yeah," he said, scrubbing his jawline, then loosening his tie. "Natalie, do you mind if I give you some advice?"

"Yes," she said. "I mind quite a bit, in fact. Especially if it's about Marc."

He blew out slowly, and nodded. "All right, then, I'll keep quiet. And if you don't mind me saying so, you're taking all this pretty well."

I'm not, she thought, but you can't see the bleeding inside.

The stenographer returned, and the next few minutes were spent rereading her statement, making one minor correction and signing all the copies."

"Do I get my picture in the paper?" she asked.

"No," Sam said. "This won't be in the paper."

"Well, for God's sake, why not?"

His face grew florid and she stepped back from his desk. "Oxrun is a small town, Nattie, and you know what would happen if we spread this all over like some kind of . . . of I don't know what. Halloween's coming up day after tomorrow. The paper comes out tomorrow. You want folks to be keeping their kids in just because some nut has a thing about the library? We have to think of the merchants, too, you know. It's a holiday."

"And suppose one of those kids in costume is murdered?"

"It won't happen."

She glared her frustration. "So, no papers. Isn't that suppressing the news or something?"

"What," he said, "do you care?"

It was time for another engagement, another round in their constant battling, but she resolutely refused to be drawn into anything she couldn't handle. Sam was beginning to frighten her.

"I'll see you soon, Sam," she said, picking up her purse and opening the door. "And please, let me know if you find out about the man that did this thing to Miriam."

"I will." He smiled blankly. "And, Natalie?"

She stopped in the hall and looked at him over her shoulder.

"I'm sorry you still don't want my protection. I don't think Clayton is going to do you much good."

"That's funny, Sam, but I always had the feeling that the police would protect me whether I wanted it or not. I thought that's the way things worked."

"Sometimes," he said, and turned away to look at the citations framed on his wall.

Evening, then, and dinner with Marc, a few silent hours in front of the television, sleeping again in separate beds.

There were no nightmares, just a few quiet tears.

For Miriam.

For herself, because she didn't know what to do, and didn't know if there was anything to be done.

The funeral Friday morning was an exercise in controlled hysteria. Aside from the silent partings, the desperate wishes that it be all part of a dream before waking, there was a caldron waiting for the right level of crying, the proper chance remark to boil into terror. The mood made skitterish instead of playful the breeze that pushed at floral displays and rode herd over dead leaves scuttling between the graves. A large contingent of Miriam's college classmates were solemn in awkward black, and their faces reflected unwitting resentment that Miriam should so violently remind them of their own mortality. Yet they prayed over their sobs and ignored the scattering of police through the mourners.

Natalie held tightly to Mrs. Burke's frail arm. The elderly woman had sought her out immediately after the church service, had stared up into her eyes for remnants of her daughter's laughter.

"You were her friend, Mrs. Windsor," the old woman said. "She had nothing but aunts and uncles. A sister, maybe, rather than a friend."

It was a lie, but Natalie refused guilt; it was enough that Mrs. Burke believed it.

And for herself, the tears had already been shed. Despite Reverend Hampton's basso requiem, she felt now a peculiar coolness, and her initial lack of emotional response had at first frightened her and made her clutch at Marc's arm until he winced and gently pried her fingers loose. But by the time the ritual earth had been scattered over the polished brown casket, she realized that the coolness was a camouflage for hardened anger. The girl she was watching condemned to a blanket of grass and marble had died in her place, and there was no remorse—instead, a terrifying hatred she'd never thought possible, and a desire for revenge that nearly blinded her.

As the crowd passed around the Burkes and pressed their hands and accepted momentary embraces, Natalie scanned their expressions for hints of complicity.

As they drifted in twos and threes toward the cars parked in the nearby lane, she watched for telltale signs of animosity cast in her direction.

"Natalie."

As they drove away in hastened procession, the only word she could think of was automaton.

"Natalie, it's been a long time."

Karl Hampton moved to stand in front of her. He was dark, heavily lined, seemingly too large for the black leonine crest over his brow. His lips thick, his nose bulbous, his eyes too deeply set to look at comfortably; worse than ugly, she thought, because ugly has its own shade of beauty. Hampton was homely—nothing more, nothing less.

And plainly disapproving of her relationship with Marc.

"Nat," Marc said softly, "do you feel all right?"

She shook herself and forced a smile tight and friendless. "Fine," she said. "Just thinking, that's all."

"She was a fine young woman," the minister said with a backward jerk of his head. "It's a pity."

"All murder is," Marc said.

"What I meant was," Hampton continued coldly, "that it's a shame one so young has to die, no matter what the cause of death. So often it seems such a waste."

Natalie was forced to agree, yet became unaccountably nervous. Everything he said had suddenly taken on variant meanings. Her death a waste? Did he mean I should be in that hole? Dammit, girl, what the hell are you doing—looking for a partnership with paranoia?

". . . and I'm sure the family appreciates your concern," Marc was saying, a careful tug on her arm starting her away. "It was really a fine service, Reverend. A fine one."

Hampton inclined his head in modest acceptance of praise.

"You will come around and pay us a visit?" he said, to Natalie only. "It seems we live so close, yet so far away from each other." He paused, but she said nothing. "I looked for you at Toal's party the other week. I was hoping you'd take a drink with me in honor of that magnificent statue." He grinned suddenly, feral and mocking.

"Somehow, Karl, I don't think you really meant that."

"Somehow, I think you're right," and his grin took on good and honest humor. "But still, I would have liked a drink or two with you. However," and he shrugged, "you have other things to keep you busy."

"Some things," she said, allowing a blush to heat her cheeks. "I keep making myself promises, you know, but I never keep them."

"Oh?" he said quickly, "you've made promises?"

"Really, Karl," she said, hating his fishing. "You did marry Ben and me, you know. At one time, then, you were rather important to my life."

"At one time," he said to Marc with theatrical regret. "At one time. You see how quickly they forget. It is the plight of the clergy, Mr. Clayton, that we are like doctors in the sense that when we're needed, we are there, and when we are not, we are as forgotten as the . . ." He looked around, seeking a completion of his analogy. "Well, you know what I mean."

Marc nodded politely.

"But, I have things to worry about, too. Please, Natalie, don't let another tragedy be the meeting for us. Come around for tea, and we'll talk about the days when you didn't know the difference between a Fox Road and a brandy alexander."

"I will," she said as he turned toward the funeral parlor's limousine.

"Now what," Marc wanted to know, "was that last remark about?"

"Not here," she said. "Let's walk a bit."

They moved aimlessly along the paved paths between the gravestones, reading the inscriptions, smiling at some, groaning at others. They made quick subtractions to discover the ages of the dead, exclaiming over pathetic youth or extraordinary longevity. The breeze geared into a mild wind, and they soon found themselves at the last row of graves fronting the lawn that spread to the hurricane fence. Through the skeleton leaves and shrubs, then, she could see the shadowed white of her house.

"Nice view," Marc said. "Now about that remark."

It referred, she said, to the time she and Ben had met with Karl to discuss their marriage. They'd found the minister in his kitchen practicing mixing drinks for, he said, his meetings with the local big shots. "They never drink anything as prosaic as whiskey and soda," he'd said, "so I have to make this . . . what shall we call it? An experiment in religious control." Natalie had tested everything he'd made and had ended up being sick over his kitchen counter.

"Quite a man, the minister," Marc said, and she pressed her arms tightly against her side in delight of his obvious jealousy.

"Hey," she said suddenly, "what do you say we get out of here?"

"Ah," and he turned slowly toward her, rubbing his hands together and leering. "My apartment, what?"

She shoved him, toppled him to the ground, and after a quick laugh at the look on his face, began running, delighting in the slap of cold air against her cheeks, blinking away the wind's tears and squealing when she heard him breathing heavily behind her.

She veered onto the grass and headed for the fence, scattering a dozen blackbirds, darting beneath them and watching as Marc moved to cut her off. She stopped, gulping, laughing, started again when he raced at her. To the fence and back again until she reached the far side of the cemetery and collapsed on a grey stone bench.

Her lungs ached, her ears burned, and when he pulled up in front of her, she lifted her hands to ward off the expected playful blows. A second, a minute, and she felt his grip on her elbows. She stood, shook her head slowly. It was not a moment of precognition, but rather a time she knew would arrive when circumstances could no longer contain themselves. She knew what he would say before his lips opened and formed the words. She knew what he would be sacrificing before his hands shifted to her shoulders and pulled her even closer.

And she wanted more than anything else to be able to say yes and pull the curtain down around them.

"No," she said. "I can't."

He didn't release her.

"I'm a danger, you know, and there's no sense in complicating things further."

"You're not telling me anything I don't know, librarian. I'm also not exactly in the best position in the world, in case you've forgotten."

"After," she said. "When we find out. Ask me again later, okay?"

He nodded, then swept a curve with his arm. "If you don't mind, though, I'll try to choose a more appropriate place. This, I think, is a little too much."

"I expected nothing more," she said, taking his arm and leading him to the gates. "You just can't do anything right, can you?"

"Oh, I don't know about that."

"You, sir, have a gutter for a mind."

"I," he said in a hurt voice, "never said anything about anything. I didn't imply, lady. You inferred."

"To the park, Marcus," she said, then laughed. "Hey, that rhymes."

"Some librarian," he said to the sky. "Marcus, park. Oh, brother!"

And, laughing loudly, holding each other tightly, they reached the front gates noisily, ignoring one or two glares and a single pointed comment about staff who get the day off for the funeral of a colleague and spend it in frivolity. The remark almost sobered her, but Natalie had known Miriam better than most, so she grinned inanely at the speaker and kissed Marc's cheek.

And once into the trees, stumbling around children already bundled in bulky winter clothes, she felt transported. Oxrun Station had vanished, and there was in its place laurel and oak and barberry and elm. Water fountains on concrete bases; wooden slat benches a peeling cold green.

A football bounced in front of them, and Marc quickly chased it down, made as though to pass it back to the boy who had come for it, then waited until he could toss it underhand.

"I never could throw one of those things," he said after the boy had returned through the bushes to the field and his mates. "I always feel like I look like a girl throwing a baseball." He mimed the stereotyped awkwardness he imagined the action to be, and she responded by slapping his back and spinning him into a tree.

"Peace!" she said quickly when he came at her, "and when the hell are you going to buy me some lunch? It's past noon, in case you hadn't noticed."

"Past noon? Then what are all these kids doing around here? Why aren't they in school?"

"Oxrun," she said, "has a little heart, you

know. Half a day so the tiny kids can do
their trick or treating before it gets dark. The
high school gets out so the brats can break
windows."

"Never," he said. "Not our sterling youth."

"Food," she reminded him, and he took
her arm.

Another ten minutes, then, of choosing
divergent paths at random, and they reached
a small pavilion squatting in the center of a
huge oval clearing. A man swathed in scarf
and leather jacket was deftly handling the
orders of a dozen or more people for hot
dogs buried beneath the sharp aromas of
ketchup and sauerkraut. Beside him, a
scrawny young girl lost in a ski sweater
slopped soda into gaily colored paper cups,
ignoring the specific requests shouted into
her ears.

"Five star, at least," Marc grumbled.

"Buy," Natalie said, pushing him into the
crowd, standing back and watching him
snatch at his glasses when a pair of boys
raced into him and nearly dumped him to
the ground. She waved at his glare, and
hugged herself, taking a strand of hair into
her mouth and chewing thoughtfully.

And when he returned, they moved away,
walking and eating, kicking at eddied piles of
leaves, lifting their heads at a flock of Cana-
dian geese crying the coming of winter.

A dirt path led them silently to the top of a
low hill, and the exposed roots of a massive,
ancient oak served as their seats. They stared

down the long, treeless slope across an open field carefully mowed. To their left, through another stand of arrow-straight pine, they could see the blue-black glints of the artificial lake where ice skating under the lights was the favorite sport. To the right, midway down the hill, was a gazebo that served as a bandstand for Sunday afternoon concerts when enough people gathered in summer to picnic and listen. And directly ahead, through the white glare of the sun just into its westering, she could see the football game and beyond, the roof of the library.

"It's like sitting on a cloud," she said, feeling as though she should whisper.

"Well, it's cold up here, if you ask me," he grumbled.

"Such a romantic," she said.

"Oh, I am that," he said, "but I'm afraid we have some things to talk about, love."

She wanted to protest, but knew he was right. After Marc's test on the road, and Miriam's death, what could have been isolated incidents of coincidence now demanded they seek out a link. Yet, again, they were restricted to suspicions only, lacking concrete evidence they could lay in front of the authorities.

"But if that's all we have," he said, "then that's all we have. So let's build us a case, and see what we have."

For an hour, then, they reviewed, dissected, prodded, argued.

A cheer drifted up from the football game,

and Natalie strained to hold it, lost it when the wind found them and infiltrated the openings of collar and sleeve.

Marc paced, toeing at twigs and rocks, kicking pebbles onto the grass. He suggested an enemy of Ben's, and she laughed without mirth. No one, she said, had ever been put away by her husband for more than thirty days.

"But you're still a target," he said.

"By what?"

"Who," he said sharply. "There is no what about this. Keep one thing in mind, love, we're dealing with people, okay?"

Grudgingly, "Okay. Then, why?"

"That's easy. There's something you know that you don't know that you know." He frowned, muttered to himself, and shrugged. "I mean—"

"I know what you mean," she said impatiently, "and I'll bet you a year's salary it starts with those missing books."

He pulled at his lips, then shoved his hands in his hip pockets. "Maybe. What kind have we got, though? If I remember right, they were the kind that needed a certain amount of thought to appreciate fully. And kinds that required faith in some type of organized religion." He looked down at her, his shadow chilling. "And you can have my year's salary, such as it is, if the replacements weren't all tripe. Crap. Shallow pieces of dreck that wouldn't strain the credulity of a five-year-old."

"Yes!" she said, standing quickly, brushing the crumbs of her lunch from her slacks. "Yes, that's exactly what they were, only I was so busy with all my other things that I never checked that closely. Boy, am I stupid!"

"Well, that's fine except we don't know why."

"Who?" she countered.

"The Council is the one that does the ordering now, you said. Toal, as President, then Dederson, Adriana Hall, Bains, Vorhees . . ." He frowned and counted silently on his fingers. "No, that can't be. See, the only reason why they'd do something like this would be to keep those who used the library in the dark about something."

"Like the college kids, who don't have one of their own," she said, picturing the dull, lifeless retreat of Miriam's friends from her funeral.

"Do you know what we're saying, lady? We're talking about an attempt to control a whole population, for God's sake! But it's too big. They'd have to bring in too many others, like Sam Windsor. I mean, you can't control a town without having the police, can you? And the commuters?" He sat abruptly on the ground and slammed his chin into a palm. "This is insane, you know that, don't you? I mean, even extending the wildest possibility that we're right, kid, who could we tell? Sam? If we're right, he's in on it. The mayor of the next town? The FBI? The President? I can see it now, just like in the old movies.

Say there ... Agent Smith or Mayor Jones
... do you know that the Town Council of
little old Oxrun Station has embarked on a
crusade to dominate its population? Do you
know that they jiggered some books, knocked
off a few folks, even sent an assassin after a
pretty young thing? How, you ask? Beats the
heck out of me."

He glared and spat dryly at his feet.

"Marc?" Natalie knelt in front of him and
grabbed for his hands. He pulled, but she
wouldn't release him, forced him to look at
her. "Marc, remember that thing I told you
about Karl and his drinks? He implied he
could get what he wanted if he knew the
right combinations they liked."

"Yeah. So?"

"He said it was an experiment."

She felt the change immediately. His hands
lost their rigidity, his lips tightened, then
parted just enough to allow a silent whistle
to blow into her face. His eyes darted from
side to side, and a slight tic of concentration
pulled at his right cheek. Freeing himself
from her grip, he pulled a handkerchief from
his hip pocket, took off his glasses and began
to polish them. Then he nodded, slowly at
first, then more rapidly until she feared he'd
break into a hysterical fit. Abruptly, however, he stopped, rose, pulled her up with
him and led her back to the path.

"Experiment," he said. "A preview, then,
for ... something. I wish I knew for what.
Natalie, if you weren't the most beautiful

woman I have ever seen in my life, I would build you a solid gold monument so the whole world would know who you are. As it is, though," he said wryly, "I am much too possessive for something that flamboyant."

"Well, I'm glad you feel that way. I think. But, Marc, what are we going to do about it?"

At the moment, he said, there was nothing they could do, no matter how frustrating their inaction would be. If they had, in fact, stumbled on some conspiracy, what they would need before anything else would be concrete proof. And still ... all they had were suspicions.

"Hounds," she said.

"Right. We've got to keep sniffing around. Circumstantial evidence is not going to help us convince some on the outside. The best thing would be to get hold of Toal, torture him, and make him sign a confession. Failing that ..." and he shrugged.

Neither, by tacit consent, tried to explain the attack on her house.

Neither mentioned the "dream" she'd had in the library.

What is it, Natalie wondered, that I know that would make someone want to get me?

And it passed through her mind that she wasn't going to be killed. Soldiers were killed; people died in accidents and during robberies and in fits of passion; people were killed by falling masonry and earthquakes and floods. It happened to them. Other people. To her—impossible. She was only a librarian in a small town more properly called a village. She was a nobody, a widow, a woman in love. Preposterous. Not her. The other guy.

They hurried, in silence, parting clumps of children, swerving only when others would not make way.

At a distant bend in the tarmac path, she fixed her eyes on a massive weeping elm held together by bands of steel to keep its forked trunk from splitting. She blinked. Put a finger to one eye and rubbed lightly. In a hollow of leaves untouched by the sun were pinpricks of light flaring like electric sparks. They were whirling about a common axis, coalescing to form behind them a shadow of indeterminate shape.

It watched her.

"Marc," she whispered harshly, "look!"

It shifted, and the leaves rustled in counterpoint to the wind.

"Look at what? Where?"

It appeared to hunch, prepare to pounce.

"There!" she said, pulling him off to the side.

Marc followed her indication, leaning forward as though to get a clearer view. Then he looked down at her. "Hey, kid, are you feeling okay?"

It was gone. She leaned heavily against him, felt an arm slip around her waist. As they passed under the overhanging branches, she shuddered and ducked her head. She felt, then, that whatever it was had not been a true threat. A warning, only.

Marc, she thought, I'm going to pack my bags and leave on the next train. You can have the car and the furniture and the house and the graveyard; I'm going to lose myself in the middle of the country.

But if she left, Marc would be alone.

"No," she said to Marc's startled look. "I'll kill him first."

"Hey! What's going on around here?"

"Nothing." She brushed a hand through her hair, lifting it to be caught by the wind.

"Good," he said, as they rounded the bend. "Then maybe you can tell me how we're going to play this miserable round."

And he nodded toward the refreshment stand clearing.

Chapter 9

DISTRACTION. OVER a dozen youngsters in football uniforms had converged raucously on the snack bar, demanding simultaneous and instantaneous attention from the harried counterman and his assistant. Freshly muddied helmets pounded against the peeling wood, and high-pitched shrieks partially covered the clatter and grind of cleats on the blacktop. Though none were more than chesthigh to Marc, their pads and colors lent them the illusion of an extra six inches. It was impossible to tell which was the losing team.

Natalie smiled at their vigor, became solemn again when she saw Ambrose Toal standing behind one of the redwood-and-concrete benches spaced at the clearing's perimeter. His gloved hands were pressed against his hips, his cashmere greatcoat forced behind him like a black opera cape. Gold-

rimmed glasses caught narrow shafts of sunlight and scattered them, and the buttons of
his houndstooth jacket were like burnished
stars as he swiveled stiffly. She followed his
gaze and saw the ramrod back of Adriana
Hall disappear swiftly around the next bend.
She was about to alert Marc, then, when he
grunted another oath, and a young woman
stepped from behind the pavilion, assisting
the owner in passing out high-stacked ice
cream cones to grasping, filthy hands. She
laughed, tousled hair, grabbed one blond
head and planted a fierce kiss on its crown.

Toal spotted them and nodded an imperial
invitation.

"We were speaking of the devil, right?"
Marc whispered as Natalie pulled him forward.

"So get it from the horse's mouth," she
muttered. "You're supposed to be a reporter,
remember?"

"But we're not ready, jerk," he said.

She ignored him. He was right, but there
was no way out. Toal was already stepping
around the bench, stripping off a pale grey
kidskin glove and extending his right hand.
She hoped her smile looked more shy than
the fear that lurked behind it.

"Mrs. Windsor, how delightful!" The show
of capped teeth beneath the dark green-lensed
sunglasses was grotesque. She accepted the
hand timidly, drew her own back as soon as
she dared—it was cold, and she tried not to

make a show of rubbing warmth back into her palm.

"And Mr. Dayton, a pleasure to see you again. Have you two been visiting the war memorial statue?" Toal was deliberately mixing up Marc's name.

Marc scratched the back of his neck. "I wish I could have, sir, but I've been out of town for a few days."

Toal snapped his fingers. "I thought it was you! You were at the conference, weren't you? Yes, of course, I thought I saw you there." He yanked off the olive ascot lumped at his throat and jammed it into a coat pocket. "Dull affair, didn't you think? I'm afraid you didn't get much for Dederson's money."

"No," Marc said carefully, "and I doubt that very much was accomplished. From what I saw, the only one not complaining all the time was you."

Toal laughed soundlessly, pointing at the reporter while he sent an approving nod to Natalie. "He's right, you know. You must have been the only correspondent not asleep." He allowed his laughter to fade, then sat brusquely on the bench, gesturing for them to join him on either side. For several minutes they watched the children scrambling for their treats, surrounding the woman in harmless vying for her favors. "Have you met my daughter, Cynthia?" Natalie immediately pressed two fingers against her lips, wishing she could see around the financier to watch Marc's expression—she was sure he was blue from trying not to gag. But when neither responded, Toal cleared his throat. "Those men are fools, Mr. Dayton," he said quietly. "Every last one of them is an unmitigated fool. They play with their money as if it were part of some childish cosmic game. Boardwalk, Park Place, take a chance and pray your luck will change. I don't know one of the old farts who isn't killing himself by working a hundred hours a day, a thousand months a year. Idiots, all of them."

"Maybe," Marc said, "but they're making their millions."

"Indeed they are. They do have their millions. But at what cost? Ten, twenty years of life because they don't know how to do it right. All that time wasted because they refuse to look for other ways to get to the same place. Like I said, they're fools."

"Well, sir," Marc said, "if they're not doing it right, what is the proper way to do it?"

A shadow interrupted them, and Natalie freed a heavy held breath. Then she lifted her face and felt it harden as expression fled inside. Cynthia Toal returned the look with a condescending nod. Unlike her father, she was dressed for warm weather. Her sun-blond hair was tied back with a wide, red satin band, her dark blouse was too sheer to properly emphasize the sunlamp tan while it over-emphasized the inadequate black brassiere, and her jeans were tight and tucked neatly into polished knee-high riding boots.

It was too much for Natalie to believe she'd chosen that outfit merely to impress a tribe of grade schoolers; and in the same thought, too much to believe that Toal normally spent his Friday afternoons giving economic lectures in the park.

Marc and Toal, meanwhile, had risen to their feet. Toal had grasped his daughter's arm, and Marc was shifting awkwardly from foot to foot, grinning inanely.

Oh, for God's sake, Natalie thought angrily, and quickly moved to stand beside him. Immediately, then, she was reminded of Elaine's and Marc's battle for possession in her room. So, she thought, the shoe shifts and all that, and she made a note to apologize to her as soon as she could.

"Well, Nat, what do you think? It sound okay to you?"

"Huh?" She blinked stupidly. "I'm sorry, I must have been in another world. Woolgathering, I guess."

"Oh, but it must have been difficult for you today, dear," Cynthia said. "I mean, the funeral and everything. There's no need to apologize, of course." She looked at her father. "But perhaps they haven't heard the news."

Toal seemed to debate before his face broke into a smile. "Well, of course not! Now that is really unforgivable of us. Here you two have been wandering the park and you certainly couldn't have been told, could you?"

"Told what?" Marc said.

"Why, about Sam Windsor, of course."

Natalie stiffened.

Cynthia laughed. "Natalie, the look on your face! Nothing bad, dear, nothing bad at all. Why," and she glanced down at her sliver of a watch, "not more than an hour ago, Sam captured the man who killed Miriam and all those other poor people."

And as soon as she said it, Natalie refused to believe it. That, she thought, was too pat, too convenient. She listened, then, as Toal explained to Marc how Sam had discovered a drifter wandering through the cemetery, muttering to himself. The old man, who must have been near fifty, was slashing out at the graves with a machete. There was a brief struggle, and Sam had been forced to kill him in self-defense.

"But we have a lot of the modern lab equipment," he said, "and Sam had them run a check on the bloodstains on that knife thing. Everything matches. Case closed."

"Now," Cynthia said delightedly, "there's no reason why you shouldn't come. It'll be a celebration, too!"

"Come?" Natalie looked to Marc.

"While you were daydreaming, Nat, the Toals were kind enough to invite us to a costume ball tomorrow night."

She scanned his face quickly, looking for signals, saw nothing but concern and nodded, reluctantly.

"Wonderful," Toal said, clapping his hands once and slipping his glove back on. "I promise, too, Natalie—may I call you that?—I promise that I won't be as rude as the first time we met. Too much excitement, and too much of that dreadful punch. I'll be sober. You can count on it."

"Great," Marc said. "We'll be there."

The sun glared in their faces as they walked. Neither spoke, either of the meeting or the news of Sam's success. It was evident in his slow and careful paces that Marc shared her doubts, that it was too good to be true. A ploy, she decided, to tip her off her guard. It would be an easy thing to check—call Sam and ask. But she knew, too, that the gist of it would be true, that Sam had killed a drifter in the cemetery, that his report would show that this stranger, for reasons deranged and unknown, had been the one who had murdered Miriam and Vorhees.

Case, as Toal had said, closed.

"Darling," Marc said when they reached her corner, "I'm going down to the office for a while." He laughed at her dismay and kissed her quickly. "Relax, only for a while. I want to write out the story I just got: Toal expounding on economics like a small-town Baruch. Dederson has wanted something like this for years, and it fell right into my starving little lap. This is one story he doesn't dare cut up."

She nodded mutely.

"I'd check on that other thing, too," he

said, plainly echoing her own misgivings. "But I gather I'm still invited to stand guard?"

Again a mute nod.

"Okay, then. And look, don't be disappointed if I'm a little late. If Dederson really likes this story, I may just stick around to be sure he gets it set for the next edition." Then his face lined and he took her hands, pressed them against his chest. "And remember, when the sun sets, lock the doors and windows. I still have the key, but I'll give you three short knocks and a long before I come in." He smiled, sadly. "I haven't forgotten, you know."

"I know," she said. She kissed his knuckles and turned him around. "So go already. And hurry! We've got plans to make."

"Like what costumes to wear?"

"No. Like what we're going to do when we get there."

She didn't have to explain and was grateful when he only nodded and broke into a trot.

She watched, took two steps toward the house and stopped. She was suddenly too restless to return home herself. There was a tempo, now, in what she was doing and what was being done to her, and she felt it quicken, like a series of waves preparing to crest.

She turned and walked back toward the library. The flag was at half mast, and there was a policeman standing at the base preparing to lower it. At the sight of the uniform, she wondered if Sam were involved in her nightmare as much as she suspected, or if, in fact, he was as guiltless as she, and the drifter, then, was Toal's doing and no one else's.

"In, out, in, out," she muttered. "I wish I could make up my mind who's in the cast of characters."

She waited until the flag had been folded and placed in the hands of the night clerk, Arlene Bains, who'd obviously showed up only for that ceremony. Natalie thought of waving, reconsidered, and continued her walk, kicking at a small pebble and unexpectedly breaking into laughter as she raced to keep it from bounding into the gutter.

"Mrs. Windsor!"

She looked up, then across the street. Mrs. Bradford was hurrying across, waving her hand.

"Mrs. Windsor, wait a moment, will you?"

Now what? she wondered. Another piece of jewelry to mortgage my soul?

The woman stopped and braced herself against a lamppost. Her face was pale in spite of her exertions, and she seemed to have trouble focusing. A hand fluttered weakly across her chest.

"Mrs. Bradford, are you all right?"

The jeweler's wife smiled weakly. "Not used to running. I keep forgetting how old I am. Fifty-four this December, you know. It's beginning to tell."

"Nonsense, Mrs. Bradford. You'll live to be a hundred."

The woman smiled at the courtesy, and beckoned Natalie closer. "My dear, I'm glad I caught you. I was thinking I wouldn't be able to tell you until next payday."

I thought so, Natalie groaned inwardly.

"You were asking me about a ring, remember?"

Natalie's eyes narrowed, snapped open quickly when she saw the woman frown. She nodded, not daring to speak.

"Well, I happened to ask my husband about it. We were at dinner the other night with the Halls at the Chancellor Inn. Have you ever been there, my dear? Wonderful place, but so noisy! It's a wonder Chief Windsor doesn't warn them. I really don't know how the neighbors stand it. And the way those young people dress! My heavens, you'd think this was Sodom instead of Oxrun Station."

"The ring," Natalie said impatiently.

"Oh, yes. Well, I asked. And what reminded me, of course, was that I saw Arty—that's Artemus Hall—wearing one just like you described. I wanted a closer look, but you must know Arty. He owns the only restaurant in town, not to mention the only bar, so he thinks he's God Almighty sometimes. And the way his wife acted, you'd think I'd asked him to run away with me to one of those hippie communes or something. Can you imagine me a hippie?" She laughed and patted her hips. "I've enough to remind me of my weight already."

Natalie forced her hands to smooth her collar, pull a strand of dark hair from her face. "Did you ask where he got it?"

"Oh, my, yes. You see, I thought if I could find out, maybe you'd think more about that bracelet we've been talking about. We can scratch each other's back, so to speak."

Natalie's lips twisted into a grin, conspiratorial and false.

"Well, no sooner did I ask him than Danny, that's my husband, Daniel, decides his ulcer is acting up and practically drags me out of the Inn on my heels. He's in the doghouse, for sure, but when he gets back, I promise you I'll find out. When I told him that you wanted one of your own—"

"You told him?" Her voice was loud, but Mrs. Bradford didn't seem to notice.

"Well, of course, dear. Anyway, when he gets back tonight from fitting Mrs. Toal for her new—"

"Oh, my God," she said. "Look, Mrs. Bradford," and she took the woman's arm and gently aimed her back toward the store, "I'm really grateful for all you've done. Honestly. Thanks a lot. And believe me, I'll be in first thing Monday morning for that bracelet."

"But Mrs. Windsor—"

"Now, I have an errand to run." She winked broadly. "A heavy date tonight, as the kids say."

Confusion vanished, and she nodded. "Of

course, and if you don't mind me saying so, it's about time, Mrs. Windsor. You're much too pretty and too young to be hanging around loose all the time. As the kids say." She laughed up the scale and without looking back ran across the street to again collapse against a post. Natalie stared after her, only vaguely aware that the patrol car had not yet left the curb in front of the library.

As she walked, she listened instead of thought. To her heels on the sidewalk, crisp and hammer sharp as the evening prepared to replace the sun and the air chilled toward freezing; to the traffic humming, snarling, reminding her of a zoo's cats prowling for a way to escape; to the thumping bass of a song that lingered as she passed a group of teen-age boys huddled around a small radio; to the crass and deliberately loud comments one of them made about the motion of her hips and the flight of her hair behind her.

She listened, turned a corner, and there was little but silence as she entered the east gates of the cemetery and headed immediately for the several rows of dark brown and grey weathered tombstones that marked the sector commemorating Revolutionary War dead and the families of the first settlers of the Connecticut hills. The markers served as a tranquilizer, a detour for her fears as she created biographies out of epitaphs and morals out of biblical quotations. At a child's grave, she knelt and brushed away the dead leaves and withered grass, passed a hand slowly over the remnants of a girl's life vanishing after two and a half centuries.

But when she found herself, a moment later, squinting to read a perfectly clear inscription, she wiped her eyes with the backs of her hands and looked up through the drab, empty branches of a blighted willow. It was dusk, and she was alone.

"Oh, confound it, woman!" she snapped. "I swear to God I need a full-time keeper."

Quickly she returned to the nearest path and followed it, the rapidly fading light altering the landscape until her sense of direction became scrambled and she found herself in an area of the vast memorial park she didn't recognize.

Dumb, she thought, really dumb. Marc is going to kill me.

She looked for the familiar to take her bearings. Only there was nothing in sight. Ordered rows of copper plates sunk into the ground, headstones both plain and sculptured poking through kempt grass like flotsam on a darkening sea. A ground mist drifted in behind the fleeing sun, tendrils that dampened her ankles and rose up the boles of ancient trees.

She ran several paces, but the slap of her shoes stopped her.

She thought of calling out, but the anticipation of panic in her voice silenced her.

Ridiculous! She had been in this place a hundred times before and never got lost—

plenty of times after dark and never failed to locate either west or east gates. Surely the path she was on would lead eventually to a main road; all she had to do was walk. But in following her own advice, she kept drifting off the tarmac onto the grass, tripping once over a toppled plastic vase. Slower, and she wondered if the stars would do her any good. Not that she remembered all their names and significations, but it was better than nothing, much better than wandering around in a circle. She held a hand up in front of her, had to stare to find its outline. Then she looked up to locate the North Star, and fairly sobbed with relief; over the trees she saw the faint glow of Oxrun's night lights.

"Follow them," she told herself, using her voice as a lantern. "You'll come to the lawn, cross the lawn and you'll come to the fence, look for the spot where those hoods bent the barbed wire posts down and you can make like a monkey and climb over. God! Will Marc skin you alive if you don't get home before he does."

Her neck grew stiff, her stumbling more pronounced as she tried to stay on the path while keeping the lights in front of her. The turns were a bother, but she managed each time to cross to another lane heading in the right direction. It became, then, an adventure more exciting than fearful, more in keeping with the relief she felt. She kept one arm stretched out before her, fending off trailing branches, knee-numbing slabs of marble, and benches that squatted just below her line of sight. Her steps grew shorter, as though she didn't want to break a leg so close to the goal.

Finally, there were no more trees, and the open expanse of lawn was silvered faintly by the rising moon. Cautiously, she moved to her right until she could see Fox Road, marked as an uninviting black corridor with its single feeble light.

"I'm proud of you, Natalie girl," she said, unable to keep a broad smile in check. "You'd make a heck of an Indian."

She took another step, and suddenly the world tilted up, rushed toward her, slammed against her forehead and stunned her into a display of stinging reds, golds and screaming whites. Her chest struck a ledge of earth that gusted the air from her lungs, and she fell backward, her mouth open, her throat working but unable to provide her with air. Tears blinded her more than the return of darkness. And when she was able to trickle a breath in, ease it out, she sat up to rub her aching breasts.

A hand went out to her side. Touched dirt. She looked up and saw stars hemmed by a rectangle. Her forehead wrinkled only a moment before her palms covered her mouth to smother a scream.

She was in a grave, freshly dug.

She was going to be buried alive.

No.

She was going to suffocate, claw, scratch her way upward but never reach the precious damp air that masked her skin, weighted her coat, softly plastered her hair to face and skull.

No!

She'd been trapped without suspecting a trap had been laid. There was nothing she could do, and no way out. It wasn't the other guy this time—now it was she who was going to die.

NO!

She heard her own protests. Biting down hard on her lower lip, she relished the taste of warm blood and the accompanying pain that made her jaw drop to free her skin. The pain, not the dying, was real. There was no one waiting to shovel cold dirt.

One more touch to the earthen wall and she scrambled to her feet, laughed aloud when her head poked above ground. An unfinished grave, not yet deep enough to keep her in. Another explosive laugh, defiant and short, and she pressed her hands on the edge and pushed, lifting herself until she could swing a leg up and over, twist and lie on the grass, staring at the stars that spread to the horizons in their millions.

Oh, my God, she thought, and filled her lungs slowly, pushed the breath out and luxuriated in the gentle sag of her chest ... rise and fall ... rising and falling ... until she felt her eyelids grow heavy.

"Whoa!" she laughed. "What you don't

need now, lady, is falling asleep in a graveyard."

She sat up, pulled her legs beneath her,
and rose, reaching out for support and finding it in a headstone.

Oh dear, she thought. Someone's already
reserved this space.

Curious, then, she leaned closer, moving so
her moon shadow lifted from the engraving.

The name was Helene Bradford's. The date
was today's.

It was, of course, impossible.

She had just spoken to the elderly woman
not two hours ago. She couldn't have died,
had the arrangements made and the grave
dug in such a short time.

Another family was the answer. Even in a
village like Oxrun there had to be more than
one Bradford; it was a common, even fa-
mous, New England name.

Nevertheless, her nerves refused to calm.
The night, she decided, was sneaking up on
her, and if she didn't start moving soon,
she'd be seeing Halloween goblins and ghosts
that didn't have little children lurking inside
them.

With her eyes steadily on the faint lights
ahead, she stepped onto the grass, her feet
scuffling to warn her of hidden rocks and
invisible, sudden dips in the ground.

A rasping sigh, a muffled snarl.

She stopped and turned, her eyes squinting
to adjust to the lack of light. But there was

only the faint glow of the tombstones reflecting the moon. Listening before turning to move again. Faster, now, almost to her normal stride.

A scratching, like a nail drawn across soft wood.

She looked back over her shoulder, refusing to stop, yet something warning her not to run. Not yet.

The sounds drifted to her right, back to her left. No closer. Maintaining a distance.

The unmistakable crunch of a heavy weight padding across the grass stiff with impending frost.

She opened her mouth to breathe in the night, her pants loud, her footsteps thundering. She began to hurry, and the stalking moved nearer; she slowed, and it fell back.

Left to right to left to right. Evenly. Toying. Cat and wounded bird. Panther and stricken fawn.

The fence split into its diamond spacing, the barbed wire slanted in toward her. If she ran now, she'd be driven to ground; if she waited, she'd never reach the fence and escape—the wire would hold her. And it was too late to try for the gates.

A hundred yards. Too far. Whatever it was, it was swift. Light-footed, powerful, muscles rippling under a black hide relaxed and unconcerned—it knew it would get what it wanted. There was no need to rush.

Fifty yards, and the distance between them narrowed.

Once again she glanced back over her shoulder. The lawn was a shimmering grey, and empty all the way back to the graves. She blinked rapidly.

Saw . . . something.

A faint luminescence, spiraling, like a dying pinwheel.

Perspiration iced her back, under her arms, trickled obscenely between her breasts. Her lips dried, felt chapped and ready to split.

She looked back to her house. Dark. Its white a mottle of black and grey. Then she remembered the damaged portion of fence, the supports for the barbed wire bent nearly perpendicular to the ground.

She told herself she couldn't do it, couldn't bear the ripping pain that would drag her back to the earth.

She told herself she had to do it.

With a slowness that threatened cramps in her arms, she slid off her coat.

Ten yards, and the sounds died.

Her shoes slipped off her feet. The grass bit coldly into her soles, and her thighs tightened.

Don't think, she ordered. Don't think. Do it!

Almost languorously, she looked toward the open lawn again, trying to gauge the distance between herself and her stalker. It was her imagination, she was positive, that produced from the spiraling red, twisting gold sparks, a puff of white breath and the lick of a pink rough tongue.

Snarling. It was impatient. Perhaps, she

thought hopefully, confused because she refused to break into a run.

The grass crackled.

With a sob, Natalie whirled and tossed her coat over the strands of barbed wire, followed the motion instantly by leaping, catching at the opening with fingers and toes and hauling herself up. She grabbed at the coat, heaved, screamed when a cuff of her blouse caught and held.

The snarl rose to an echo of hatred.

She heaved again, frantically, toppling over the wire head first.

Something crashed into the fence, rattling it like chains in a deserted dungeon. Her wrist throbbed and her shoulder ached where they'd taken the weight of her fall, but she ignored the pain as she leaped to her feet and dashed up onto the porch.

And the door was locked.

Marc!

She screamed once, was answered by the thing backing away to hurdle the fence. Again she screamed and ran down the stairs, darting around the side of the house. Tripping over the concrete lead at the base of the gutter. Driveway gravel gouged into her hands, ripped at her knees as she crawled desperately to the garage and yanked at the heavy doors. They resisted and she kicked at them with her stocking feet. A scrape, and one gave maddeningly slowly. The fence shook as the thing passed over and, heedless of the splinters slicing into her back, she slid inside the windowless building and hauled the door closed.

There was darkness.

There was a thud against the wood.

Another.

And another.

She dropped to the dirt floor and put her head in her lap, her arms crossing over the back of her neck.

A sniffling at the tiny gap between doors and drive, a snorting and a pacing that circled the garage while she rocked herself on her haunches and crooned. Spittle slid from the corners of her mouth. She licked. Licked again.

And the pacing became a frenzied race, a frustrated charge to find an opening where none existed.

And when she realized she was safe as long as the bar across the doors held, Natalie began to laugh.

Chapter 10

DARKNESS WAS absolute. Like suspension in black water. Sitting was floating, nothing to give her a sense of perspective, a grip on that which was real. She had stood, briefly, but not being able to see had made her dizzy and she quickly crouched to the floor again.

When sensation at last returned and her hysteria had spent itself against the garage's coarse, unpainted walls, her arms and legs danced in a violent trembling she was powerless to control. She rode it like an unbroken horse, hugging herself until first her legs, then her arms calmed; and the cold began a sifting through her skin, up through her buttocks to her spine, penetrating her sleeves and collar. A nauseating mixture of oil, gasoline and damp earth, dirty rags and dead grass made her stomach lurch, and she bent over, retching dryly while her throat protested and tears scoured her cheeks.

She sat. Thoughtless. Refusing the speculation that would batter down the conscious barrier she'd erected against her terror.

She raised an arm, turned her wrist, but the watch's radium dial was blank.

At last cramps forced her to straighten her legs, and she massaged her thighs, reached down to rub hard at her ankles. The burning of her palms against the rough texture of her stockings was vaguely pleasing and she worked harder, kneading her flesh until she could remove her hands and still feel radiating warmth. To her arms next, scrubbing, gasping once when a nail jabbed into her bicep.

And the sound of her gasp made her freeze.

But the garage was silent. The sniffling was gone, the thunderously persistent race around the small building apparently ended. Faintly, then, the drift of a whining truck. She angled her head, trying to follow the anchor as long as she could; and when it was gone, she nodded and prepared to consider her alternatives.

It was obvious that whatever had been sent to her was not immaterial enough to pass through the concrete; it had its limitations. So long, then, as she remained inside, she would be safe until Marc returned home. But until that time, she would have to do something to keep from freezing to death.

Carefully, she rose to her feet. One hand stretched out before her, slowly scything the air while she rotated on her heels. A complete circle had no interruptions. A sideways step to the right, and she began again. Another step, and her fingers met cold metal. She sobbed aloud and threw herself against the Olds, draping herself over the hood and caressing its smooth curves. She kissed it once, laughing, and found her way to the door, opened it and clambered in. The seat was cold but she didn't mind; she twisted over the headrest and fumbled until she found a blanket folded neatly in the corner. A moment later it was settled around her shoulders, and she inched out from under the steering wheel to the passenger side, thumbed open the glove compartment and allowed herself a gasp of pleasure when her fingers curled around the flashlight Marc had left there.

The light was dim, but enough to make her turn away until her eyes adjusted. It was a weapon against the night, and she directed it into all the shadowed corners, nodding at every twinge of recognition until her cheeks ached from her smiling. A check of the car's interior unearthed no traps, only the stains and smudges and tears and dents of too many memories to sort out in a lifetime.

Then she slapped herself on the forehead. "You idiot!"

She leaned over and fumbled under the dashboard, gnawing her lips until she felt the familiar rectangle of a magnetic keycase. She cursed when it eluded her grip and fell to the floor, and the flashlight punched white holes until she recovered it, freed the key and inserted it into the ignition.

She hesitated. News stories about people trapped in their garages with the motor running, asphyxiated by carbon monoxide. She tried to picture the walls, the doors, any place where there might be a crack to permit the invisible poison to escape; and she sat behind the wheel in frozen indecision while tears of frustration gathered again.

She pounded the wheel with impotent fists, and then blew on her hands to keep them warm. Finally, with numb fingers, she turned the key.

It coughed twice before catching, and she drummed her nails on the seat beside her, counting the seconds by one thousand and one until, flicking on the fan, a gust of warm air exploded into the car and made her applaud.

She held her hands under it, shoved her feet under it and rubbed them together, sighing at the pricking the cold left as it retreated. Then she rolled down the two front windows; she knew it would partially defeat her purpose, but caution dictated she suffer an ounce of discomfort in payment for a guarantee of the future.

This, she thought as she leaned her head back, must be what it's like to be rich.

And as she was drifting into a light-headed doze, she heard someone shouting. It was probably Marc, and he was probably wondering what she was doing sitting in the car in the middle of the night in this garage. She would have to get up. She would have to open the door and step out onto the dirt floor. No. The dirt was cold. She didn't want to be cold again. She would wait until Marc came to help her. But he couldn't, of course. The doors were bolted. She would have to get up. She would have to open the door and step on the floor and walk across the dirt to unbolt the doors. But Marc was clever, and he could figure out a way to get inside without having to use a door. There was no window, but she was too tired to move. Her legs were so comfortable . . . and the seat was warm . . . and the blanket was just beginning to feel cozy and soft . . . and Marc would have to wait until . . .

There was a pounding. The shouting was louder. Disturbing her sleep. Angry now. Marc was really very nice, but very inconsiderate.

The pounding increased, the bar rattled loudly. She could hear her name and it sounded quite pleasant. Natalie. A nice name. Natalie. Nice. But not the way Marc was yelling it. What will the neighbors think, for God's sake?

She roused herself and slid out of the car, falling against the hood and dropping to her knees. There was a roaring in her head apart from the engine's grumbling. She clutched at her temples, but the roaring refused to be banished. Using the car for balance, she pulled herself up and when she reached the end of the fender staggered into darkness until she fell up against the doors.

Move the bar, she told herself. And she sagged against it, asking just a little nap to regain her strength.

Something struck the outside, and she jumped back, cursing inaudibly. She threw up the bar and the door jerked away from her. There was light, a white light off to her right, and in front of her a man grabbing her arm and pulling her outside.

"It's cold," she said, tripping over a trailing corner of the blanket. "It's cold."

"You know," Marc groused, "this is getting to be a pain in the neck. I mean, every time I get to spend the night in this place, it's because you've gone and done something to scare the hell out of me. One of these days, lady, you're going to drive me to buy one of those blow-up dolls to cuddle with."

Natalie listened to his complaints, felt the sheet beneath her and wondered how he managed to get her undressed without taking one or two small pinching liberties here and there. The idea made her grin. She had told him everything, and the flush that darkened his forehead had intensified to an angry red. He made her drink a warm brandy, then followed with dark steaming tea. He rubbed her arms and legs, and bundled a fresh blanket around her until she looked down and thought she saw a mummy lying in her bed.

A single lamp glowed in the bedroom's corner. Quietly. A child's nightlight, while he sat on the edge of the mattress and held tightly to one hand, toying absently with each of her fingers in turn.

"Well," he said finally, reluctantly, "I hate to say this, old kid, but I think the battle's been joined."

She closed her eyes in agreement. "Who?" she asked in a small voice.

"It's obvious now, isn't it? I mean, especially after today? You don't think Toal invited us to his soiree just because he likes my reporting, do you? He's head of the Council, he makes all the decisions. It's Ambrose Toal, Nat. Toal, his daughter, Adriana and all the rest of them. They have something they're using to—I don't know what the right word would be—produce, I guess, this thing that comes after you at night. You, and the others who weren't so lucky."

Toal, she thought; I have an invitation to my death.

"But why do I get away?"

"A warning the first few times, I think, or however many times it happened, or was close to happening. Tonight, though," and he reached to the nightstand and picked something up, dropped it into her lap. She gaped, but her hands would not move. It was Ben's ring. "You had it in a pocket of what was left of your dress."

"I went to the den this morning," she said

quietly, as Marc retrieved the ring and returned it to the nightstand. "I was going to throw the shoe box away. I guess I just dropped the ring into my pocket. Marc . . ." She looked up, but he was staring at the wall, at something he did not like.

"Nat, I want you to pack up and get out."

It was said. And she hated him for saying it, even though it was the natural thing to do. She hated him because she almost agreed, despite her earlier convictions to stay and fight.

"Drink your tea," he muttered.

"If I keep this up, I'll be spending the whole night in the john."

He struggled against a smile, and lost.

"And I'm not leaving," she said, groping for his other hand. "If they're all that anxious to have me . . . dead . . . why will moving away solve anything? If I don't die here, I'll die in another town. And . . . they do want me dead." It was strange how calmly and rationally the words came out. *They do want me dead.* "Not you, though. Not yet. That's why they only, somehow, hide Oxrun from you."

"Maybe before," he said. "But not now, I think. I have a feeling I'm on their list."

"Don't!" She squeezed his hands until he winced and pulled them gently from her. "Wait a minute," he said. "Let's go downstairs and get something to eat, do you mind? I don't know if I can take all this in as fast as you seem able to."

There was only a moment's vacillation before she threw aside the blanket and reached for the robe he held out to her. Embarrassment held her hand a second longer than was necessary, and when she saw him grin, she shook her head. "Is that all you can think of?"

"What? That you could stand to lose a pound or two?"

He exaggerated an examination of her figure while she slipped her arms into the sleeves, then ducked when she spun with a slap aimed at his head.

"Ye gods!" he yelled as she chased him into the hall and down the stairs. "How I manage to control myself is beyond me. It must be because I don't like taking advantage of dumbbells."

At the foot of the stairs he grabbed the post, spun, slipped, and fell heavily against the wall. He sat, legs poked out in front of him, and Natalie straddled them, hands on her hips.

"What time is it?"

He checked his watch. "Nine-thirty."

"Brother, it feels like two in the morning. What do you want to eat?"

"In the kitchen, preferably," he said.

"Don't get smart, reporter," and she held out a hand to pull him up. "Just march."

They had soup and grilled cheese, afterward carrying their coffee into the living room. Natalie studiously avoided the sofa, preferring to have the porch windows at her back rather than having to search the shadows for signs of whirling sparks. Then, while Marc tossed his jacket onto the floor and kicked off his shoes, she ran back upstairs to the bedroom and fetched the ring. When she returned, he was sprawled, throw pillows lifting his head, his cup on the rug by his trailing hand.

She held up the ring, tossed it to him. "All right," she said, "the link. I just wish I knew what ... what powers it had, or if it's only a symbol of whatever it is they're doing."

"Well, it's obviously more than a symbol, isn't it." He closed his eyes, his brow lined until he nodded and looked at her again. "Good. Fine. You saw it on Sam and on Bains. Have you seen anyone else with it that you haven't mentioned?"

"No," she said. "Just those two. But Mrs. Bradford told me that Artemus Hall was wearing one, too. And from the way she told me, I wouldn't be surprised if her husband has one. There's no question that Toal has something like it. Maybe the first one, if there was a first one."

"Yeah," Marc said, a mirthless grin on his face. Natalie did not like the look and glanced away, saw darkness in the corners of the room and held her breath until she was sure they were only shadows from the lamp. Take hold, kid, she told herself; then, take hold or you'll be screaming your lungs out.

"How many of them are there?" she wondered aloud, more to herself than to Marc.

"I don't know," he said. "It's like a membership card, though. And obviously something more." He held the ring in his palm and rubbed at it vigorously with a thumb. "Oh well, no genie," he said. "And, as far as I can see, no cabalistic writings on the inside." He poked at it with a nail. "It doesn't open, either. The Borgias would be disappointed."

"All right, Marc, but—"

He sat up suddenly and waved off her exclamation of surprise. "But me no buts, as the man said. Whatever it is, besides being a pretty ugly ring, we already know it's the thing that's been protecting you all this time, right?"

"I guess so."

"Come on, Nat, use your head! Whenever that beastie has tried to get you, you've been near enough to the house to cut down on its strength. For God's sake, if it's powerful, *real* enough to tear a man apart, then it sure could have come through those glass doors upstairs that first night."

"But tonight—"

"I already told you, Nat. Come on, you're losing your grip and that isn't going to do either of us any good. Tonight you had it on you, and it's the only thing that kept it from . . . from doing you in. Whoever sent it must have been awfully mad to make it get as close as it did. You weren't near the house when the library thing happened, but that was, as I said, just a warning."

"Warning," she said softly, thinking of Miriam.

"Right. Whoever directs it can't see through its eyes. He, or she, just says I know where that woman is, so go there and get her. Mystery number one therefore solved—the ring is what they're after."

"Why didn't they just break in when I was out?"

"Because they didn't know you had it. Not until you started with Mrs. Bradford. That tipped them. Now they know."

"Then," she said, wondering why she felt so coldly calm, "mystery number two—why do they want it so badly?"

The telephone rang, cutting off his answer. She rose, but stayed by the chair when Marc lifted a hand. "It's them," he said, sudden confidence in his voice. "Checking to see if you're dead."

The word was as obscene as any she'd ever heard.

"But what if it's Sam?"

"What of it? He has a ring, doesn't he?"

"But you said the police—"

"What I said and what I now know are two different things, love. Answer it, and give him a heart attack."

The corridor extended, and she felt as though she were mired in a tunnel at the end of which a train waited to run her down. In the kitchen she could only stare at the phone on the wall.

"They won't wait forever, love," Marc whispered in her ear. He reached over her shoulder and handed her the receiver.

"Nattie? Nattie, is that you?"

She stammered something, hearing only Elaine's nasal twang.

"Nattie, Sam's out at cards again and I thought you and me could have a talk or something. To pass the time, you know?"

"I'm sorry, Elaine. I have work. It's important."

"Oh, I understand. I just worry about you, you know that."

"Yes," she said, her mouth dry and tasting of ashes. "Yes, I know."

"You've heard the latest, I imagine?"

Natalie tipped the receiver so Marc could hear, leaning on her shoulder. She mouthed a name, and he nodded.

"Yes, I did."

"You did?" Elaine sounded incredulous, and Natalie couldn't help a dry grin.

"News like that travels fast, Elaine."

"Oh. Yes, well, I guess it does. Helene was such a good woman, too. Heart attack, is that what you heard?"

"It was." Then, suddenly, she said, "Elaine, will I see you tomorrow night?"

"Well, of course, you—"

"Good! What will you be going as?"

A silence, and Marc patted her head, kissed her lightly on the shoulder.

"Going as? Going as what? To a shower?"

"Oh," Natalie said, willing to play the role. "I'm sorry, Elaine, I thought we were talking about the same thing. It doesn't matter, though. As long as you get out of the house once in a while, right?"

"Right," Elaine said, doubt clouding her voice. "Right. Well, Nattie, I have to go now."

"Oh, sure," Natalie said, and hung up without saying good-by.

Marc led her back to the living room, easing her into the armchair before perching on the window seat behind her. She could hear his heel tapping lightly against the wood.

"She's foul."

"Books and covers, Nat, books and covers."

"Helene didn't have to die, Marc. She didn't have to get involved."

"You weren't the cause, Nat. Don't kid yourself."

"No, I was. I was asking about the ring. I saw her gravestone tonight. She was already marked, probably from the day I first brought it up to her. She only made it faster when she pushed Hall about it."

She listened to the tapping, leaned back and closed her eyes. She marched, then, from point to point since Marc had become involved in the ... she struggled for a word. Plot. Yet there was still that one major question to be answered, one gap to be bridged. The key was in Toal's hands; and the only way she was going to find it was to show up at the party nobody had thought she would be attending.

When she told Marc, he whistled a long, respectful note. "God, you're some kind of woman," he said. "I was going to suggest that before, but I didn't know how you would take it."

"Marc, if I don't—we don't—we'll be spending the rest of our lives running inside this cage they've built for us. We can't go to anyone on the outside. This is real; and real people don't believe in what's happening to us. We have to do it, or we'll be running. For the rest of our lives."

There was pressure on her shoulders, and she reached up to touch Marc's hands, lifted her head to press a cheek against his fingers. When he moved to pull her up from the chair, she held him tightly; when he buried his hands in her hair, she sighed. He stroked her back, reached down and unbelted the robe; she shivered once as he kissed her, lightly, then fiercely.

It was dark. Light. A failure the first time as tension held her back and made her weep with frustration. He whispered, cajoled, made her laugh at herself while he uncovered the pockets of resistance and gently caressed them into oblivion. He exclaimed, wondered, praised. Natalie watched as the texture of the room's darkness softened from one of funereal veils to warm, engulfing velvet. She responded, laughing, and held his head against her breasts and wept again. Silently. Thankfully. Whispered an answer to the proposal he had made only that afternoon.

Afternoon.

How many years ago had that been? How many people had died, been buried, had been marked for burial because they had discovered the secret of Oxrun Station. Empty and full, she scratched his back lightly, giggled at the catlike purring muffled in her chest. All those automobiles, trucks, buses, drifters, oblivious to the village that had set up a screen of trees and sleepy inaction.

"Marc?"

"Hmmmm?"

"Do you think Elaine is really a part of this thing?"

"Who wanted you to visit a psychiatrist when you weren't taking Ben's death as well as a so-called normal person would?"

"And Sam?"

"Do you really think all that protection was because he cared about you? Or because he wanted to keep an eye on you?"

Order in the Court. Mrs. Natalie Windsor, plaintiff, accuses Mrs. Elaine Windsor, defendant, of involvement in a plot to murder her, drive away her lover, and control the population of Oxrun Station for reasons unknown, unsubstantiated, unbelievable. Isn't it true,

Mrs. Windsor, that the death, the violent death of your policeman husband caused you a great deal of mental anguish? So much so, in fact, that your closest friends consistently and futilely advised you of the necessity of visiting a professional counselor who would assist you in regaining your touch with reality? Isn't it true that you refused to seek this assistance? What do you have to say in answer to those who have testified as to the state of your mind during this year and a half since that tragedy? They are your friends, Mrs. Windsor. You should have listened to them.

"Marc?"

"Hmmm?"

"Do you believe in the supernatural?"

"Ghosts, you mean?"

"I think so."

"No. Not ghosts. Something else, maybe, but not ghosts."

"Then . . . it isn't Ben coming back?"

"No, don't be silly. Not Ben. He was part of it, Nat. He had a ring, too, remember? Not Ben. Something else."

The radio communication the night Ben died. She replayed it, and finally caught the words in that last frantic exchange. *Don't believe it . . . it isn't . . . have to shoot . . . oh, my God! . . . promised, he promised . . . oh, my God, Sam!* Not that he didn't believe what he was seeing; he didn't believe that what he was seeing was coming after *him!*

He had done something, jeopardized the plan, and had paid for it. He was part of something and never said a word to her. No wonder he didn't care about the promotion Sam received instead of him; he had other plans. Greater plans.

"Nat?"

"Hmmm?"

"Nat, the way this is going now, when they learn we know what's happening—or, rather, when they think we finally know what's happening—there's going ... Nat, we may have to kill somebody to protect ourselves. Somebody may have to die to end this."

"Are you asking me if I can do it?"

"Yes."

Conceivable. That, if the Oxrun plan succeeds, it may spread to other, larger communities, towns that will vanish slowly but inexorably from the sides of highways and turnpikes, towns that will turn away drifters, or murder them, and incorporate themselves into something increasingly more powerful. And someone else like Miriam or Helene Bradford or the man with the dirty coat will have to die because they didn't know, or in knowing didn't believe until it was too late.

"Marc? I can do it. I'm not sure. When it comes to it, when I have to face it, I may change my mind. But right now, if you ask me, I can do it."

"You are one fine, remarkable woman, Natalie Windsor."

"Clayton, stupid. Natalie Clayton."

When the sun rose, she was lying against his chest, and in her dreams a panther stalked.

Chapter 11

*T*HEY DECIDED their Saturday was best played normally. Marc reasoned that suspicions could twist into action unless they were able to convince Toal and the others that, though they might be confused, they were still innocent of the enormity of the plot. It would be better, at least, than hiding in corners waiting for the sun to go down.

"I'm going to go to the office."

Natalie pouted as she poured him a second cup of coffee. But the reaction was unreasonable, she thought, since she had decided to put time in the library to make up for Friday. It just seemed to her to be more natural that on a Saturday Marc should stay in the house and do whatever it was men did on their days off.

"Dederson," he explained then. "I left the preliminary article on his desk last night, and I want to see if he's read it yet. It could be a big break."

"It will be," she said, sitting opposite him. "Listen, you're pretty good, you know. You don't have to worry about losing your job. That old creep doesn't dare let you go."

"If I'm so valuable, how come I'm not making twenty grand a year?"

"You're too young. You need seasoning."

He laughed, touching her hand as he emptied his cup. "Seasoning is for poultry. Money is for people."

"Do you really care all that much for money?"

His face presaged another jest, but he pushed back his chair and stood. "No, kid, not really. I've done without it this long, I don't think I need all that much. Besides, I already have what I want."

"Gold digger."

"Oh, sure."

She grinned. "I mean, dope, that Cynthia Toal would have you in a minute if you let her."

"Her? Hey, I'd be a full-fledged eunuch ten minutes after the ceremony. I'll bet she has a collection of scalps a mile long."

"Go to work," she ordered. "Call me when you get a chance."

"You'll be careful, right?"

Immediately, her mood darkened slightly, but she shook it off and nodded. "I'll be as normal as ever. And believe me, I'll be careful."

"All right," he said. "As long as you're—"

"Confound it, Marc. Will you please get out? You're making me nervous hovering around like that. Go! Call! We'll have lunch if I can get away." He hesitated, bent and kissed her cheek. "I could easily get used to this, you know," he whispered.

"So get used to it, already. Get going!"

And after he left, she filled the kitchen with sound, humming melodies of songs long forgotten, clattering the dishes in the sink as she ignored the washer for a little exercise and the comforting sting of hot water, the scrape of furniture, the slap of a rag as she dusted briskly.

Upstairs to change: a ruffled blouse promising glimpses of her breasts; a dark green suit with a skirt Miriam would have been proud of; a matching cardigan to replace her ruined coat Marc had retrieved from the fence. She considered piling her hair into a bun, decided instead to allow the auburn a chance to fight with the sun.

Walking, then, in a world of altered perception, seeing the Station from an angle unthought of before her troubles began and the nightmare became real. The Pike and its one-way traffic, the businesses on Centre Street—just the right proportion of low-cost and privileged establishments to keep the inhabitants from straying too far for their needs. For those who worked within Oxrun itself, it was entirely possible they could attend their entire lives without breaching the village limits.

The old men were on their benches, and she paused to kibitz a while, returning their smiles and tolerance with such good humor that several had to look away in embarrassment.

A police car drifted by, and its grey-and-white was an alien thing, like a shark passing through quiet coral waters on its way to a distant, leisurely kill.

Whoa! she told herself, be cool, lady, be cool.

The library was unusually busy, with hordes of children in the stacks searching for stories like the ones their teachers had told them the day before the holiday. Many were already in costume, tramps and princesses and a smattering of skeletons with wrinkled black between the faded white bones. There was a huge crystal bowl on the main counter, filled with single-bite bits of candy, and Arlene Bains seemed hard pressed to keep track of those who were returning for thirds and fourths. When Natalie entered, she looked up with a plea for help, and Natalie couldn't resist a sympathetic smile.

"Boy," she said, taking refuge behind the horseshoe, "you've got fans today, haven't you?"

Arlene's characterless face flushed. "I could do without all this nonsense, you know. A pagan adjunct to a Christian parody, that's all it is. Garbage." And she turned away to swipe at a hobo whose sticky hands were reaching up over the desk.

"Charity, charity," Natalie muttered.

"Charity, crap!" Arlene said. "Look at the way they go for that tooth-rotting stuff. It reminds me—"

"Arlene, please!" She fought an impulse to call her a Scrooge, and didn't want her to spoil the clouds of laughter and squeals the children rose to the vaulted ceiling. "But I'll say this, libraries were never like this in my day."

"Or mine," Arlene agreed, and Natalie quickly left before there was an acid qualification.

There was little in the office to occupy her for more than a couple of hours, and after she'd placed the last letter in its envelope, the last voucher in its file, she stood by her rear window and looked out over the pocket park in the back. There, too, the old men were stationed with their reds and blacks and sculptured instruments of intellectual warfare. By standing as close to the pane as possible, she could look down onto the parking lot and see Adriana's station wagon solitary in its special slot.

An impulse grew. She wrestled with it, called it foolhardy and dangerous; it would serve no purpose except to aggravate further antagonism.

"Oh, well," she said as she left the room. "You only live once, right?"

She stood outside the Director's office,

fussed with her clothes—pulling the ruffles aside with a self-satisfied grin—and knocked lightly on the door, stepping in without waiting for a summons.

Adriana was standing by a bookcase on the right-hand wall. There was a glass in her hand, empty, and in the other a faceted decanter of amber liquid. When Natalie walked in, she looked up, startled, and her face paled, her lips pressed tightly together and vanished.

"Good morning, Adriana," she said with as much sickening sunshine as she could muster. "Do you have anything for me today? There was less than I thought piled up after yesterday."

"You, uh, weren't supposed to be in today," Mrs. Hall finally stammered. "I mean, I was under the impression you were going to take the day off."

Natalie shrugged. "It's better than sitting home feeling sorry, Mrs. Hall. I mean, life does go on, you know."

Adriana recovered slowly, covering her confusion by replacing glass and decanter and taking her place behind the protection of her desk. She shuffled through some papers, setting aside some, placing others in a pile in front of her. Then she sat and folded her hands tightly.

"Natalie, I've been meaning to talk to you." Her voice had recaptured the actress timbre her surprise had smothered, and Natalie felt the pleasure of confrontation on her terms slipping rapidly away. "Natalie, I'm beginning to wonder—and only wonder, mind you—just how suited you think you are for the position you now hold."

Attack and counterattack. The tactic was obvious, but that didn't stop her temper from champing. "If you wish me to be as objective as I can be, Mrs. Hall, then I would have to say that I'm about as qualified as anyone for my job. At any rate, more so than anyone now working in the library."

"I thought you'd say that." She opened her hands, refolded them and leaned heavily on her forearms. "You see, the Council is considering a further cutback in funds due to the state of the economy. Not only in the country, but in Oxrun itself."

'And you seem to think they're looking for ways to cut staff without cutting efficiency. And that would seem to me to indicate that a director can handle anything on the administrative level, without an assistant."

Adriana let the supposition pass without comment. She lifted a pen from the center drawer and began doodling on a pad in front of her. Natalie watched silently, wishing Marc were there to see this new phase of attack; chip away at the anchors that held her to the Station, and once cut off, elimination would be easier and far less conspicuous. And she didn't consider it at all unlikely that Bains had been poring over her bank statements looking for a loophole in the mortgage.

It should have been dismaying, but Marc's fierce keenness for the hunt and engagement had transmitted something of itself to her, and she felt a decidedly uncharacteristic exhilaration. There was no such animal as a strategic advance to the rear. Grant's dictum to Lee, instead: attack, and attack again. Bangs, not Eliot's whimpers.

"Have you nothing to say, Natalie?"

"What can I say, Mrs. Hall?" She shrugged an attitude of no concern. "If you're going to eliminate the position, then eliminate the position. If not, why worry me with uncertainties? It's not, if you don't mind my saying so, the best way of breaking the news to me."

"I would just like you prepared in case of the eventuality."

"And how eventual is it, Mrs. Hall?"

Adriana made as if to rise, thought better of it and leaned back in her chair. "How eventual? I really cannot say, but I had hoped you'd take it in the spirit in which it was given and start sending out queries so you won't be without an income for very long."

Natalie backed toward the door. "Mrs. Hall, I do take it in the spirit that you gave it. And I don't want you to think that I'm not grateful."

"That's all right, Natalie." She smiled without emotion, and the result was a death mask. "I just want to help you. You mean a great deal to me, you know. More than I usually allow my employees to get."

"I'm flattered." She opened the door behind her, turned, then looked back over her shoulder. "By the way, was that what Ambrose Toal was telling you in the park yesterday after the funeral? That I was going to be eliminated?"

Adriana opened her mouth, shut it tightly and glared. "You've made an error, my dear. I'm afraid I wasn't near the park yesterday. Miriam's services quite overwhelmed me. All those people ... I didn't think she had so many friends." Natalie spotted a sudden slip in the mask, a tic at the corner of her mouth, a slight increase in the rise and fall of her chest. "I was overcome. I didn't know. No," and she shook her head. "No, I went straight home to bed."

"My mistake, Mrs. Hall. I'm sorry. And, by the way, I'll be leaving around four today. Is that all right with you?"

Adriana nodded. Natalie watched her silently for a moment, then closed the door quietly and stepped to the railing to look down onto the lobby. Arlene was bustling behind the counter, a parttime college girl constantly bumping into her as they struggled to make up for Miriam's leaving. The girl moved dully, as though in sleep, and Natalie rubbed her chin thoughtfully. Then she hurried down the sweep of stairs and headed back into the stacks. In Arlene's hand she had seen a portion of a printout, but

Natalie didn't think she needed it anymore; she was sure she could remember enough to make a quick conclusive check.

She and Marc had been right. The missing titles had not been repurchased. The replacement books were bland and innocuous, and she had to search for over an hour before she found a single volume on religion of any kind other than paganism and myths; it was a slim book on comparative studies tucked into a dusty corner out of place and obviously long forgotten.

She thought of Sam's sudden aversion to blasphemy. Of Arlene's reaction to the children's Halloween games.

She wandered, her eyes skimming titles until they blurred into a sameness that made her dizzy. Her stomach rumbled, and a little girl sitting cross-legged on the floor looked up and giggled. Natalie smiled down at her, mouthed *I'm starving*, and moved into the next aisle. Automatically, her hand dusted along the spines, feeling the weight of the words behind the raised gold, the swirls of color, the simple designs not hidden by dustcovers. Her neck developed a tightness as she scanned the upper shelves and she paused, rubbing, face down and not seeing the carpeting or the tiny pockets of dust and lint that had gathered at the green metallic bases.

She froze.

Her left hand pulled at her waistband, and

she turned to see who was watching her. But the library was still frantic, Arlene still occupied with children and the incompetent girl.

Slowly, then, she knelt. On the bottom shelf was a book, shorter than its companions, and thinner, bound in nonreflecting black. On the spine near the bottom was a silver embossed shield, within which were two red dots split down the center by a silvered erratic line. She reached out a hand, yanked it back and brushed it nervously along her thigh. Again she reached out and touched the book, gingerly, waiting for some arcane expression of hatred at her discovery. Beneath her finger she felt the grit of accumulated dirt even though the book itself appeared to be new. It resisted her first attempt to draw it out. Stuck, she thought, and withdrew her hand. The voices behind her took on a curious buzzing quality that tickled her ears. Her knees complained, and she snatched at the book, yanking it out and dropping it onto the floor. The front cover faced her. Blank. Except for the center, and the red and silver.

She didn't want to touch it again, but it would be foolish to leave it, though she didn't know exactly why. Biting at the inside of her cheek, she lifted it as though it had bristles dripping instant poison, then grabbed at a shelf and pulled herself up. The buzzing grew louder. She shook her head and rushed back to the stairs, paying no attention to Arlene's sharp calls for assistance.

But another woman's voice made her grip the railing tightly before she was halfway up; and, tucking the book out of sight by her hip, she looked down and saw the clerk suddenly deferential, practically fawning over the attention of a customer in a tight-fitting sable coat. At first she thought it was Cynthia, but the bearing was too stiff, the voice too deep, and a lift of her head identified her as Ambrose's wife. She mumbled something, and Arlene nodded, jerking her thumb up and behind her. Instinctively, Natalie looked up at Adriana's door. Mrs. Toal immediately snapped at the temporary assistant, scribbled something on a scrap of paper and shoved it into her hand. At the same moment, Christine looked up and smiled into Natalie's stare.

Reaction was automatic; she inclined her head only enough for the acknowledgment to be seen, then forced her legs to carry her up to the gallery. She stopped at her door, turned, eased back to the railing and saw the girl return empty-handed. Saw the frown on Mrs. Toal's face and the simpering bend of Arlene's back.

Through the level of noise that rose toward her, Natalie heard one word clearly: *mistake*.

Bingo, she thought.

She didn't bother to clear her desk of its clutter; rather, she arranged things purposefully, setting pen and note pad close at hand in case she should be interrupted. Then she dashed off a few words on the top page so that anyone looking down would think she was in the middle of a letter.

The book lay in the center of her lap, below the level of the desk's top. Carefully she opened it, flipping past the end pages. There was no title or mention of copyright or publisher. On the first page, one word only: EYE.

On the second page, a single sentence: *There is nothing the* EYE *cannot see when properly directed.*

The third page: *To direct the eye, open the lid; to open the lid, call the* NAME; *to call the* NAME, PREPARE.

And the fourth: *There is no time in the light of the* EYE.

Gibberish, she thought, disdainful and disappointed. Gibberish in a private printing on a private press. She read on, turning the pages rapidly, seldom finding more than a dozen words on a page, the contents of which were neither difficult nor profound—a patchwork thesis, apparently, of a philosophy not referred to by name, not given a title, possessing no tenets other than the vague references to something called the Eye. At first, she was reminded of personal dynamics clinics which assured success through inner improvement and the encouragement of overwhelming confidence. But reflection had her decide that this had been written by someone who needed a justification for wealth unworked for, an insecure individual who was searching for a label on which he could paste a reason for affluence that otherwise might vanish like a fog before the wind.

Self-indulgence, she thought, and was about to toss the book onto her desk when she turned over a page-large sketch of the cover's design. This time, however, the two dots and wavy line were done in broad strokes within a broken-line outline of a head. It was definitely feline, though the ears were less pointed and stretched back toward its neck. The cheekbones were higher, the mouth more human than animal. She stared, letting her imagination color it in, fill it out, and what she saw was the menace of her nightmares.

Impossible, she thought, but the reaction was weak. A demon? But no mention anywhere of Satan, Pluto, any one of the familiar underworld denizens, no talk of covens, caldrons, sacrifices to the rising sun.

She leaned back in her chair, felt it give and present her with a view of the ceiling and its acoustical ripples and rills. When she had problems to sort out, she would wipe her mind clear of extraneous thought by mentally connecting what lines she saw, forming pictures in the ceiling much like children form images out of clouds. This time, however, all she found was the face of the cat.

"All right, then," she whispered. "Read on, and find the spell to conjure that thing."

But when she again located the sketch and

turned the next page, it was blank. As were all the others, nearly fifty of them.

"Now this is dumb," she said. "This is incredible."

Anger made her hands tremble. She returned to the beginning and reread, trying to find depth behind the words, the symbolism in the phrases.

And by two o'clock she had given up. She slammed the book into a drawer, reached for the phone and called the *Herald* office. Marc, however, had left at noon to have lunch at the Inn with Dederson. No, the woman who answered said, she didn't know when they'd be back but yes, Dederson had seemed excited and Marc was in better humor than he'd been in weeks.

"At last!" Natalie said to the empty room. Now if he would only appear to wave a magic wand that would solve her problems as well.

She blinked.

A noise, rising, striking a hysterical pitch and subsiding almost instantly. The sound separated itself as she stepped around her desk, and she realized she was listening to, had been hearing but paying no attention to an argument in Adriana's office. She pressed her ear against the wall, but the words remained indistinct. She glanced at her door; hesitation was minimal and she moved swiftly to the gallery. The library was still crowded and a quick check over the railing assured her Arlene and the girl were still ensconced behind the counter. Then she moved back and stood by the paneled door, nearly stumbling back when she realized it was not closed all the way, and the voices were clear above the noise from below.

"I don't care what you think! I don't care! Not anymore. It's too much and I—"

"Jesus Christ, put down that glass!"

"And don't talk like that in this room. If you're going to use language like that, you can get out now."

"You are insane, you know that? You are really, absolutely insane. You sound like that disgusting cop, for crying out loud. And who do you think you are, giving me orders?"

"Please, Christine, don't talk like that. I . . . I'm just confused. The girl—"

"Forget the girl. She's dead. Period. No loss. I have more important things to worry about just now. Like where you put that book!"

"Christine, you must be deaf. You must be. I've said a million times I do not know where the hell that book is, and if you don't stop asking me, I'm going to scream your goddamned ears off."

"You do not know. Just like that, is that right? You do not know. Well, listen, my dear, you had better know. And you had better know by tonight. Ambrose is going to be awfully annoyed."

"Christine, you can't tell him!"

"It's always interesting when Ambrose gets

annoyed. Of course, sometimes he only talks a lot. On the other hand . . ."

"Oh, my God, please! I don't know. It was there, and now it's gone."

"Tonight, my dear. She is going to be there, you know. And this time there isn't going to be an end until there is an end."

A silence. The clattering ticking of glass against glass.

"You know, I'm beginning to think perhaps you don't belong with us, Adriana."

"Christine, don't say that. Not ever. Never say that. I've done a lot, you know, and you can't talk to me that way."

"Very well, I'm sorry."

"You don't sound it."

"I am not accustomed to begging, Adriana."

"I'll find the book, believe me. That girl you sent me probably moved it."

"She's doing just fine. Don't blame your mistakes on her."

"Fine, ha! Are they all like that out there now?"

A rustling, then, a shifting of cloth against leather.

"Some. It affects them in the beginning like that. But they do get over it."

"Well, I hope so. There have been complaints."

"It will pass, Adriana. It will pass."

Another rustling.

"I will drop in later to see—"

"I'll find it, I'll find it! Now will you please get off my back?"

Natalie scurried into her office and eased the door closed, her hand tight on the knob until she could engage the catch soundlessly. And despite the sunlight and closed windows, the room seemed cold, the trees outside brittle and ready to shatter at the first breath of wind. She backed away until the desk prodded her legs and turned her around. A palm touched the desk's top as though she expected it to be stove hot.

It was all true.

All the speculations and half-formed theories about conspiracy and control, all of it true and the key was the book she had hidden in her drawer.

The book, and the ring.

She was twice a target now.

She giggled, sucked in her lips to stifle the sound.

Twice a target: the book, because it has some value as a guide to Toal's power; the ring . . . she shook her head, plucked at her blouse.

And uttered a startled scream when the telephone rang.

Chapter 12

"IDIOT!" SHE whispered, and clenched a fist to calm herself. A glance at the door to see that it was still closed, and she lifted the receiver, pressed it against her stomach. A deep breath and a hand across her forehead.

"Nat? This is Sam."

She pinched herself to keep from bursting into tears, cursing the weakness that shoved her continuously from decision to indecision. Then she pushed her hip hard against the desk.

"Sam, what can I do for you?" Just the right amount of pleasure at hearing his voice, yet sufficient professional overlay to indicate she was otherwise occupied and didn't have all day to gossip.

"Nat, I've been thinking about Ben."

His voice was strained, an oddly heartening sound.

"What's the matter, Sam?" Sympathy, now; and it was bitter on her tongue.

"I was doing some checking of the things you gave me." He chuckled indulgently. "Elaine didn't much care for those trophies and things in the house. They sort of made my own contributions to fame kind of puny."

Get to the point, she thought. "Well, I doubt that, Sam. More likely, she was just jealous."

"That I can definitely say she was, Nat."

"Well, what's the problem? Don't you want them anymore or something?"

"Good grief, no, nothing like that. I was just wondering, though, if . . . well, this is going to come out all wrong, see, so I don't want you to get mad, okay?"

"Get mad? What for? He was your brother as well as my husband, Sam."

"Fine. Good. I'm glad you see it that way, Nattie. Maybe I should just say it out straight and you can take it, hopefully, the way I mean it, okay?"

"Okay. Whatever you say." The game was wearing thin, and with a glance at the wall, she suspected what his next question would be.

"Well, I was wondering, Nat, if you ever . . . well, of course, you clean the house and all, but in doing things like that, I wondered if you ever came across anything of Ben's that you didn't want." A pause not long enough for her to interrupt. "I mean, I don't know if you would ever throw anything out, Nat— "

"Not without talking with you or Elaine first, Sam."

"—but maybe you found something that you just stashed away and forgot. I was kind of thinking of him the other day, you know, and I'd hate to see anything of his lost. You know what I mean."

"Sam, you're worrying about nothing. I do clean the house once in a while, you know," and she laughed to prove she hadn't taken his prying as intrusion. "And I haven't found anything more. It was all cleaned out after the funeral. All of it."

"Well . . . I don't know . . ."

"Sam! Do you mean to tell me you think I'm holding something out on you?" Another laugh, while her right hand picked up a pencil and jabbed its point fiercely into the desk. It snapped on the third try, but she continued to punch with it.

"Don't be silly, Nattie, but . . . remember when you came to my office a while back? I showed you a ring I said I'd admired on Ben? Well, I might have given you the impression that it was his ring that I had."

"You didn't, Sam. You said you had it made, remember?"

"Great! I'm glad you do remember. What happened was, I got to thinking maybe you knew where his ring was. I was talking to Elaine the other night, see, saying that it was really stupid of me to go and have this thing made and pay all that money when I could have ... well, could have been wearing Ben's. It would mean a lot more, if you know what I mean."

"I know what you mean," she said. "I know exactly what you mean."

"Natalie, are you all right?"

She looked down at the hand gripping the pencil and shook her head; then she cautioned herself with a slight but painful jab at her leg. "I'm fine, Sam. It's just been a hard day. Everyone's rather tight around here. Miriam Burke and all. And there's a ton of kids in for free candy, and folks are gobbling the books like they were calories. It's been a strain is all. You don't sound so good yourself, in fact. I would have thought you'd be flying high because you captured that murderer."

"Oh. Well, of course I'm happy and everything, but it's never fun killing a man. Even if he was crazy."

"Was he?" She knew her voice sounded hard, but it was all she could do to keep from screaming out her hatred. "Was he really crazy?"

"As a bat."

"Sam, I've been wanting to ask you—"

"No, Nattie, I don't think so, if I guess your question. He was just a drifter. It would have to be some coincidence for him to have been here that long ago. I think maybe he just heard about it somehow, and being crazy, well, he ... you know."

"Yes. I guess I do."

"Well, fine, Nat, and I'm glad you're okay. And you're sure you don't have the ring."

"Never found it, Sam."

"He wasn't—"

Sam, she thought, what do you want from me?

"No, he wasn't buried with it. Only the wedding ring."

"Oh. Well. It was just a thought."

"And I appreciate the thought behind the thought. I know you loved him a lot." And you didn't have to say that, you idiot, she told herself. Knock it off before you get caught with your symbols down.

"Okay, Nat. And look," he said as she was taking the receiver from her ear. "Nat, you still there?"

"Yes, Sam. And don't worry. If I should come across it, I'll bring it right over. I wouldn't know what to do with it, anyway."

"Okay, kid. Thanks a lot. And hey, I'm sorry to bother you like this. I guess it still kind of hurts to talk about it."

"No," she said. "Not anymore. Not for a while."

She listened, heard nothing until the line broke and the dial tone shrilled.

So, she thought, Marc was more right than he knew when he said the battle had been joined. And the opposition was working itself into a mild, dangerous panic. A missing book, a missing ring; the former was still her secret, but the latter she was positive they knew about, if only because they hadn't been able to kill her yet. If only she could decipher what more there was to that miserable piece of jewelry.

"You're just going to have to be patient," she whispered to the silent telephone.

Patience, however, was beyond her. She called the *Herald* again, but Marc was still out. Then makework occupied her for the next hour, finally drove her to grab her heavy sweater and leave the office. At the gallery's top step she paused, then retraced her steps to Adriana's room, knocked and went in.

Mrs. Hall was seated behind her desk, staring out the window. Natalie stood silently for a moment, then coughed discreetly into a closed fist. The Director didn't move, and Natalie frowned. A quick check of the office revealed nothing in the way of violence that might have erupted after her argument with Christine, nothing at all except an empty decanter.

"Adriana?"

The woman remained still.

"Mrs. Hall?"

She stepped farther into the office, then dropped her coat on the leather couch and hurried around the desk. Adriana's face was pale, drawn; her eyes were open, but there was no reaction when Natalie passed a hand before them. She picked up her right hand and fumbled until she located a pulse, slow but regular. The woman had passed out, and neither a good shaking nor a shout directly into her ear could bring her out of it.

"You know something," Natalie said, hands on hips, "I think you're more frightened than I am, lady." And she was calmed.

She looked around the room, then rolled the wheeled chair to the couch. Without insuring much against bumps and bruises, she pushed and prodded Adriana from her seat onto the divan and took off her shoes, loosened her buttons at her throat. Two fingers lowered her eyelids, and when she left there was the faint but unmistakable sound of snoring.

"Don't tell me you're leaving already," Arlene called to her before she reached the bottom step.

Natalie shook her head and moved over to the desk. "Just saving myself another trip upstairs. I have until four today." And she dumped her wrap at the end of the horseshoe.

"Nuts," the banker's wife said. "Don't tell me I have to lock up."

"Sorry about that, but I have things to do. Meanwhile, what's new?"

And while Arlene grumbled, she leaned carelessly against the counter and checked each of the library's visible alcoves and specialized areas. The children had gone; there were still several adults browsing around the magazine racks and in the stacks. But the old men had deserted their benches, none were inside. Arlene saw the direction of her glance and snorted. "They said it was getting too cold. Next thing you know they'll be taking over all the reading rooms. I wish Mrs. Hall would just keep them out."

"Why?" Natalie said. "Where else are they going to go? The police station?"

"Oh, forget it," Arlene snapped and grabbed for the Fine Book and the electronic calculator.

Touchy, Natalie thought, checked the clock on the wall, and began to wander, straightening a book here, replacing one that had been stuck back incorrectly. For five minutes she crawled on the childrens' section floor poking around for a missing puzzle piece, and found it under the lid it had come in; she picked up three plastic covers without magazines, two scarves, three mittens, and an empty coin purse stuffed with candy wrappers—these she carried over to the desk and dropped into the lost-and-found drawer with all the other articles discarded and forgotten. She asked where the new girl had gone, and Arlene muttered something about hunting for a stolen book, a best seller they'd gotten in the day before. Natalie only nodded.

Five minutes before four, she heard a door slam and saw Adriana weaving from her office to the washroom.

"Okay," she finally said, fishing in her purse for her keys and tossing them in front of Arlene. "My time's up. I'm free and I'm going. Have a good night."

"Will I see you later?"

Natalie paused as she was turning away. "Later?"

"At the Toals'. Weren't you invited to that costume thing tonight? You know, witches and ghosts and all that."

"Oh. Well, as a matter of fact I was. Yes, I was."

Arlene smiled at her for the first time that day. "What are you going as, if it isn't a secret?"

Natalie was about to say she hadn't given it a thought, but an unbidden image crossed her mind and she grinned back. "The first woman monk."

Arlene scowled. "I don't know that that's appropriate, Natalie."

"Why not? It's a costume, isn't it?"

"Well ..." She was obviously goaded to say more, but tightened her lips and tested the desk's drawers, their harsh rattling a loud reproof.

Keeping her left hand tucked into her pocket where she'd stuffed the book when she left her office, Natalie waved an abrupt good night and hurried outside.

It was cold, the sun already below the horizon and gradually pulling the light after it. Frost was laying streaks of glittering white on the benches and grass. There was no wind, and for that she was grateful as she trotted to the corner and waited for a break in the traffic. The shadows that followed her to Fox Road seemed too fragile for even a leaf to land on safely.

At the corner she decided to walk to the newspaper office and surprise Marc with company on the way home. Her spirits had been buoyed after her exchange with Mrs. Bains, her mind reeling with variations she could have played, and she was almost beyond the church before she heard someone calling her name. She stopped, looked behind her, then across the Pike to the rectory where Karl Hampton was standing on the lawn, beckoning. She waved, would have gone on, but he moved to the sidewalk and stood there, waiting.

"Now what?" she muttered as she crossed the street.

"Natalie," he said, taking her right hand strongly. "I'm glad I caught you before you got away from me again."

"Oh," she said, "should I be flattered, Karl?"

He seemed confused, then released her hand and tucked his chin toward his chest. "Well, I don't know about that, Natalie—"

"Oh, come on, Karl! I was just kidding. You always take things too literally, you know that?"

"No, I hadn't known that," he said seriously, frowning as though considering the consequences of what she'd said. "No, in fact, I've always—"

"Karl, come on! What can I do for you?"

"Do for me? Why, nothing, Nattie." He looked up again and stood with legs spread and hands clasped behind his back. He gazed up at the belfry and released, slowly, a deep, long breath. "I was just going through some old books of mine—the parish register, you know—and I started thinking about you and Ben and your wedding day."

"You and the rest of the world," she murmured, then waved off his quizzical look. "Nothing. I was talking to myself."

"Oh." He accepted the explanation without pursuit and returned to a contemplation of the ravaged remains of his church. "Well, I was thinking about that day, and I wondered if you do, too?" His smile was guileless, and she shook her head.

"Hardly ever anymore, Karl."

"Oh, that's a shame."

"I don't think so. I mean, he's dead eighteen months now, and I have other interests."

"I know." He began a rocking on his heels. "I've seen you in his company."

Now this is the limit, she thought. "Karl, you're not going to warn me against Marc, are you? Or maybe you're just looking for the rights to the service."

Hampton ceased his rocking and swiveled to look down at her, his face hard with displeasure. "Nattie, you know I have only your best interests at heart. Since you were married in my church by my hand once, I think it behooves me to see that you don't get hurt."

"Nice ring," she said, nodding at the hand tugging at his white collar. "Ben had one like it, you know."

No word games here as he snapped his

hand back out of sight. "I don't want to keep you from your appointment, Natalie."

"Thanks, Karl. It's still a nice ring."

And as she strode away, grinning, she heard his heels following, turn aside and snap up the walk to his front porch. Deciding she had already made it tough enough for herself in whatever was coming, she resisted the temptation to turn around and wave. She only wished she'd had an opportunity to tell him about the monk's costume; it would have been a delight to see him strangle on his fury.

The *Herald* plant was empty except for a woman sitting just in front of Dederson's office. Natalie stood at the door, waiting to be recognized, then wove past the desks and asked how long it would be before Marc returned from his afternoon meeting with his editor.

"Oh," the woman said, "He's come and gone, Miss . . ."

"Mrs. Windsor."

"Oh, yes, Mrs. Windsor." No judgment, only a filing for future reference. "Well, he came in around three and ran right out again. He said something about running up to Harley for half an hour."

"Harley?" It was a fair-sized community some twenty miles up the Mainland Road, and she wondered aloud why he had to go there without calling her first.

The woman shrugged. "Don't know why,

ma'am. He just ran in and out. You know how he is."

"I'm afraid I do. Well, would you tell him I was here? And to call me as soon as he gets back? I'd appreciate it."

"Sure."

Natalie hovered, hoping the woman would volunteer something more, but when it was evident the conversation had ended, she headed back to the door, stopped at Marc's desk. There was a pad in the center of his blotter, and on it, two dots with a straight line bisecting the space between them; beside the design, an exclamation point, and the letter D.

Dederson had a ring. And why not? Considering the news he allowed to be printed and that which he arbitrarily suppressed, it shouldn't be at all surprising. And it eliminated the final source for independence Oxrun had, the last true link with the outside world.

She stepped outside and gasped at the slap of cold damp air rushing across the fields opposite the Pike. She shivered and drew her sweater close to her throat, grateful that the thick Irish wool was nearly as warm as her lamented gold coat.

Her eyes watered in the wind, looking at but not seeing the slow procession of automobiles filing into town.

Harley. Dederson had sent Marc there; to get him out of the way while something was done to her? No, there had been too many missed chances already. That the trip might possibly have been legitimate was given even less credence. But when the solution came, it was nearly a physical blow, and she raced across Mainland to check the road bed north and south. If things were indeed coming to a head, getting Marc out of Oxrun would insure his not returning simply because he wouldn't be able to find it.

She began to run. The gravel scattered along the shoulder made footing precarious, and several times she slipped and went down to her palms. Gusts from passing trucks shoved her into the ditch between road and field. She slowed. No cars were parked on the shoulders in either direction, on either side of the highway. She glanced at the deserted fields now overgrown with brown, dying weeds, dotted with stands of trees shorn of their leaves and bleak against the graying sky. A ground fog sifted through the wild shrubbery that served as fencing, licked at the bottom of the ditch and stretched up toward the road. Automobiles drifted behind yellow lights, and buses already had their headlights on, blinding her in the last glow of twilight.

She swore loudly and stumbled to a halt, using a telephone pole to rest against until her breathing came easier. Its rough exterior was a comfort, and she stroked it absently as she sought for a way to keep from panicking, wondered how she would be able to identify her car when the last light vanished. Her ears began to sting, and a dull ache blossomed at the base of her skull. The dampness had become frigid, and she didn't discount the possibility of the season's first snowfall before the night had ended.

Suddenly she spun around at the screeching of brakes and the frightened blare of several horns. The southbound traffic was veering off the road to avoid collision with a car swerving erratically from lane to lane. Natalie watched, then moved to put the pole in front of her, and shouted once as the car straightened and aimed directly for her. She ran back, slipped and fell into the ditch, her hands skidding painfully into pockets of stone and gravel. Scrambling she tried to scale the opposite side, darted a look over her shoulder and saw the vehicle as though in slow motion: sliding off the road, spewing stones into a black wake behind it, striking the telephone pole and shearing off a great bite of wood before righting itself and returning to the highway. Within moments after it vanished, it was as though it had never happened. The traffic closed upon itself and kept on moving.

"I don't believe it," Natalie said, sitting on the lip of the ditch. "He never even stopped!"

Too shocked and angered to succumb to a reaction, she touched her pocket to see that the book was still with her, then brushed her hair back from her face before returning to the shoulder, conscious now of the mud and grass clinging to her legs. She swiped at them ineffectually while staring up the road, shaking her head and hoping somebody would stop at the nearest phone and call the police. And as she stood, staring numbly at the pale gap in the pole where the car had struck, a flashing red light intruded and stopped several yards north of her. The headlights were painfully glaring and she raised a hand to block them. She could hear the motor, blinked against the spinning red. But no one left the car.

It idled. Like a beast waiting. Nothing but the steady white, the hypnotic whirling red.

"Come on," she muttered. "You have to come here."

Abruptly, her legs weakened, and she clung to the pole. A van hissed by, light spray dotted her calves.

The patrol car grumbled.

Then the passenger door opened and a dark figure slid out, stood by the fender. With a resigned sigh, Natalie pushed off her support and walked carefully, picking her way across the gouges the careening car had dug.

"Natalie, what are you doing out here?"

She closed her eyes and swallowed a sudden surge of bile. "My God, Sam, did you see that guy? Did you see the way he was driving? He must have been drunk, Sam. He nearly killed me."

Windsor shook his head. He wore a heavy blue jacket, and his arms were folded across his chest. "I saw nothing, Nattie. I tried to contact you at your house and there was no answer. I thought maybe you'd gone for a walk."

"Well, obviously I did and nearly got killed in the bargain."

"I wanted to protect you, Nattie, but you refused me. Remember?"

She took a step forward as he tugged at the peak of his cap, and with the light now at her side, she could see his face. He was staring blankly, without condemnation and completely without concern. It was so unlike him that she instinctively bunched the sweater at her neck and tugged nervously on her purse strap.

"I want you to come back with me, Nattie."

It was the emotional vacuum more than his look that made her refuse.

"Natalie, you're being foolish."

"I'm waiting for Marc," she said finally, hoping she sounded more confident than she felt. "He's up to Harley for a story. He'll be back any minute now."

"You always wait out here?" and he swept an arm toward the ditch. "You don't want to be in another accident, do you?"

"Hey," she said, "what is this? Don't you have to report damage and things like that to the telephone company? I mean, don't you have to call in?"

"Nattie, you're tired. I think you ought to let me take you home."

She turned away suddenly and headed back down the road. Sam followed, his boots scattering the gravel as if he was kicking it out of his way. A piece struck her ankle. Then she faced him, pointing. "There! Now what are you going to do about that? Couldn't you at least radio or something to try to catch the man?"

Sam brushed by her and examined the pole closely, his cap shoved back on his forehead. "Catch him? For what, Nattie?"

"For what? What are you—" She grabbed his arm and pulled him around to the front of the pole. "See? For nearly killing me and for ..." Her voice faded. There were no marks in the wood. She turned. No skidmarks on the road, no disturbances in the gravel. She bent over, her hands running over the side of the pole, prodding for weaknesses, searching for traces of car paint. But there was nothing. Not even a chip missing.

"Sam," she said tightly as she stood, "I was standing right here! And there were cars scattering all over the place. It hit the pole here!" And she punched at it twice.

Sam nodded, rechecked the pole, then took her elbow. She pulled back, but he was too strong to resist. "Come on, Nattie, I'll take you home."

Too confused to speak, she balked as much as she could, feeling his grip close tighter in anger. She slipped once and was yanked painfully upright.

"Now wait a minute, Sam, I'm a big girl, you know. I can find my own way home. You don't have to do this, Sam!"

He kept silent. When they reached the

patrol car, he opened the rear door and stood aside, gesturing impatiently. She resisted, flinging her arm back and out of his grasp.

"Natalie, please get in the car. I'll take you home. You'll be safer there. Much safer."

"Safer for what?" she demanded.

But before he could reply, a car pulled up behind them and its lights blinked off and on. Windsor spun around, cursing, and Natalie used the distraction to race past him.

"Nattie!"

She opened the door and looked in, nearly sobbed when Marc grinned back at her.

"Trouble?" he said.

"I love you," she said, her breath coming in spurts.

"Nice place to tell me," he said, then frowned over the steering wheel. "Is that our Sam out there?"

She nodded. "Wait a minute." Then she waved back toward the policeman. "It's okay, Sam, it's okay now. It's Marc. He'll take me home. I'm all right now."

"Are you sure?" The presumption had vanished, and what she'd begun to think of as the old Sam temporarily returned. "Are you sure you'll be okay, Nattie?"

"Fine," she said. "You go on doing whatever it is you do at night. I'll be fine."

"Just be careful, Nattie," he said as he backed into the patrol car. "I don't want you wandering around in the dark like this. You could be hurt. It isn't good, Nattie. You could be hurt."

"I almost was."

"Natalie—"

"Good-by, Sam," and she slid into the car and slammed the door. When Marc automatically bent over for the emergency brake, she held up a hand to stall him. The police car waited in front for just over a minute, then barreled onto the highway, heedless of the traffic, gravel from its spinning rear wheels spitting against the Olds' grille. Its taillights vanished into the mist as she rubbed her feet under the heater's warm blast. Marc's silence soothed, and when she leaned her head back on the seat, his hand gathered in both of hers and squeezed. Her eyes closed, and the tears finally found the way out, stinging her cheeks where the cold still pricked. Her hair felt heavy, pressing her skull more firmly into the vinyl, and the ache expanded to furrow her brow.

"I went to the office," she said as he pulled carefully onto the road. "A woman there said you'd gone to Harley."

"Almost," he said. "Until I figured it might be a way to keep me from going to the party tonight."

"I saw your sketch."

"Pretty, wasn't it? Toal's got them all. Every one of them."

"Yeah," she said. Then, "Slow down, Marc, the traffic light's up ahead."

He leaned toward the wheel and shook his head. "I can't see it at all. Nothing but road straight to Canada."

"All right," and she talked him into the turn, nervously as it left Mainland, relaxing only when he sped up the Pike.

And it was sudden. In the silence she felt as though she was a child, small and vulnerable to the attacks from an adult world she didn't understand. Where rules should have been, there was only Toal; where people should have been friends and lovers and comforters, there was only hostility and a sinister blacking of the soul; and nothing at all was as it should have been.

Her arms pressed to her sides, and she felt the book stiff against her hip. It would be so easy, she thought, to take it out and tear up the pages one by one and dump the pieces into the gutter. It would be so easy, and then I could die and sleep and never feel tired again. So easy. So . . . easy.

"Natalie?"

"Hmmm?"

"You still want to go?"

They swept by the church, its stained-glass windows eternally dark, the mold on its stone black and shimmering in the starlight.

"Yes," she said. "And I've got something for you to read."

Chapter 13

ᚪT WAS a strange shade of melancholy that settled on Natalie's shoulders as she rode toward the party, a melancholy that hinted at a grieving for the death of a holiday.

September grade school, and the cutouts the teachers would have them paste in the windows, of pumpkins and witches and moons with great shining faces; the burned cork on her nose and cheeks, the over-sized jacket her father had unearthed from some cob-webbed trunk in the attic; the pillow case for the candy, the apples, the gleaming new pennies.

High school, and the parties where she and her friends had made unknowing fools of themselves sipping at contraband beer, nearly drowning while bobbing for apples, had spent the darker hours in bravado fearful gropings toward their first sexual experience.

The horror movies that flooded television,

the gimmick films that opened in theaters, electric shocks and three dimension and canvas skeletons that clanked on rusted rails over the heads of the audience.

It had been a night for taking salt with the supernatural, and allowing the shadows to frighten as much as they had the children.

But it had always ended with the coming of the dawn.

This time, however, nothing would end. No matter what she and Marc accomplished at the mansion this night, no matter what force/power/horror they met, Halloween would always be now the hour of the Oxrun dead.

She wore her caftan again, with several alterations suggested by Marc and her facetious comments to Arlene in the library. The hood was up now and draped carefully over her face. On her feet were heavy wooden sandals Ben had fashioned when they'd been the vogue. The wide white band had been replaced by a length of new clothesline, and her hands she tucked into the voluminous sleeves Mandarin-style. Around her neck, a black braided cord from which hung a gift from Marc—a fair-sized gold ankh that weighed heavily against her chest.

Marc had taken some sheeting from the linen closet and with several safety pins and a deft hand with a needle had managed to create a passable toga, this too with a hood. "It was the custom of the Romans, according to the gospel of Shakespeare," he said when she questioned the addition, "to throw the hood over their faces when shame came upon them."

"And are you shamed?" she'd asked.

"For not throwing you into bed instead of doing this? You're absolutely right I am."

They had spoken little since leaving the house. There was no plan, no course of action—he had insisted they only keep their eyes and ears open and look for an opportunity to search the rest of the house; in spite of what they knew, they knew too little and anything else would lay them open for too many mistakes.

"There must be something in that book," he said, making her jump. She glanced at his face reflecting the dashboard's glow, and it gave him lines and hollows she wished she hadn't seen. "In the mansion, maybe."

"What do you mean, invisible writing? We already held it up to a light and over the stove."

"Well, maybe not that exactly, but I can't see wasting all those pages for nothing. The thing's too important, obviously, and all that crap in the beginning about opening the eye and directing the lid and like that ... there's something missing, definitely."

She reached out to press a hand to his stomach where they had strapped the book; that it would be used as a last resort as a bargaining point for their lives did not make her feel the least bit comforted.

"You'll be careful, right?" she said as they turned into the private lane.

"I will if you will."

"Oh, well. Into the fray and all that jazz."

"All for one, and us against all. Or something like that."

"Don't," she whispered, and leaned over to kiss his cheek. "I love you."

"You've said that already. Don't go spoiling me into thinking I'm some kind of superman."

She gave him a smile she didn't feel, gasped when he opened the door and she stepped into the cold. Her prediction of snow was fast becoming a reality. The stars and moon had vanished, the mist had lifted to give halos to the lights on the veranda, and her breath puffed in front of her like the fleeing of a soul.

The butler greeted them solemnly, a ludicrous contrast to the explosions of revelry blasting from the front room. Masks were laid out on a silver table in the center of the hall, and Marc chose two—black for her, white for himself. When he slipped the elastic over his head and adjusted the eyeholes, he leaned close to her ear and whispered, "You'll never guess who I'm supposed to be."

"Fine, then I won't bother," she answered as she donned her own mask. Then, their hoods settled to cover the upper halves of their faces, they walked arm and arm into the party.

"Oh, my God," Natalie said in amazement. "If the Masque of the Red Death comes walking in now, I won't be in the least surprised."

"You," Marc said, "are a prude."

He led her across the massive room, threading his way between pirates and ghosts and Egyptian queens, Lords and football players and Adam and Eve with only their leaves. The women were either overdressed or pinkly, fleshily straining for the erotic; the men were flexing what muscles they had, unashamed of the preponderance of middle age that bloated their waists and sagged their breasts. All were masked, all were drinking, and their faces beneath the stiff plastic bands were grotesquely incomplete. They swirled around a huge barrel in which Natalie saw apples floating, and the aroma from the dark liquid told her one bite and she'd be drunk for a week; they screamed laughter at a game of pin-the-tail-on-the-donkey, where the donkey was a woman and the tail her nipples. The walls had been stripped of their portraits, replaced by speakers sounding the clarion of a band in the adjoining room, and lights that glared in no discernible patterns; they were in fact the only sources of illumination.

"Look," Marc shouted, and pointed above them where she could see huge fish nets holding back hundreds of balloons and rainbow streamers. "For the unmasking at midnight," he added unnecessarily.

"I don't think I'll live that long."

A Satan rushed up to them, carrying a tray of champagne glasses. Marc accepted for the both of them. "Drink up, Father," he said with a grin. "You've got dispensation for the night."

"Cheers," she said and emptied the glass, then grabbed Marc's hand and followed him into the next room, a mirror of the first but twice as large, and had on the back wall a kaleidoscopic slide show whose theme, Natalie decided when her breath came back, was sex in the sixties, fifties, forties, and any other time they could have fornicated in front of a camera.

"Brother," Marc said, "will you look at that?"

Natalie laughed and pulled him away. "You try it and you'll have cramps for a year."

"Yeah, but what a way—"

The words were lost in a renewed burst from the band. Natalie turned until she was dizzy, but couldn't locate the musicians; there was dancing, but only where there was room and the inclination; singing along, but only when someone didn't order the singers to move someplace else.

"Food," she said suddenly, the noise beginning to reach down and drag up her headache. "Come on, lecher."

Marc stopped ogling a glistening Amazon and reluctantly joined her at a table set against the east wall. Several times on the way they were questioned, but cautiously, the rules seemingly against revealing identities; and from her cover under the hood, and the way guests seemed to shy awkwardly away from her fingering of the ankh, she was able to observe without too many interruptions.

"I have this feeling," Marc told her as he pressed a brimming plate into her hands, "your costume is going to be something of a wet blanket hereabouts."

"Are you complaining?"

He grinned, then lowered his head so she had to lean close. "No, Nat, but we're both too easy to spot. I wish I'd known handkerchiefs were going to be the uniform of the day."

"Don't worry about it," she said, squeezing his hand, and he smiled and stuffed an olive into her mouth.

For an hour they wandered the four connecting rooms of the party, Natalie too stunned by the noise and growing abandonment to reply to his comments. She was hot, and perspiration was making her squirm as it trickled down her stomach and legs. Several times she had to lean against a wall, feeling the thudding bass from the speakers pound into her spine. The lights made her eyes sting, but she couldn't avoid them, couldn't escape the spastic shadows their frequency spawned. A fight broke out between a Beau Brummel and a Musketeer, neither of whom could stand on his feet for more than a couple of swings; they ended the brawl leaning back to back and toasting the legs of a feathered chorus girl. She blessed them mockingly.

Finally, Marc pulled her into an unoccupied corner. "Hey, I haven't seen anyone, have you?"

She shook her head. "There are so many people, though, I don't know. I thought I saw Hall a few minutes back, in some kind of white hunter thing."

"No," Marc said, "I don't think it was him."

He pushed back his hood and rubbed at his hair, the ends damp and plastered darkly against his skin. Then he pointed toward the front. *Now or never*, he mouthed, and she allowed him to lead her through the crowds, past the drunken groping of a hundred hands, the one startled yelp of surprise when a Hercules discovered she was a woman.

Once in the hall, now as crowded as the rest of the first floor, they maneuvered toward the stairs, climbed and leaned for a moment against the top railing.

Like children we'll be, Toal had said in the park. Some children, Natalie thought.

The corridor was much less pressing. Couples and singles drifted from the rooms whose doors remained opened, and through one Natalie saw the setups for gambling. At the end, she nodded to her right. "That's where I hid in that room," she said, and lifted a hand to mop the perspiration from his face. He grinned, and kissed her palm.

"Maybe," he said, "we should go the opposite way, just to check."

"But why go blind, Marc? I think we ought to start with what we know. What I know, anyway. We go down there and we could get ourselves lost."

Marc turned to look back at the stairs, and the guests who ignored them. "Okay. You lead the way, MacDuff."

Slower now, they passed under sconces with imitation gold gaslights. The sounds of the party had dimmed, and she guessed most of them had moved into the back rooms, away from the windows that looked out onto the cold. She stumbled, and Marc snared her wrist. The light was dim, as though they'd breached a grey veil. The shadows were hazy, and the ceiling-high drapes that masked the rear windows in dark greens and browns moved sluggishly as drafts pushed weakly from behind.

"Where?" Marc asked quietly, and she tried to remember which of the heavy paneled doors had been her salvation the first time. The first or the second: each was twenty feet apart, and she didn't run that far, didn't recall having the time. She chewed on a fingernail, then pointed to the second. Marc nodded, puffed his chest with a lung-clearing breath and indicated with hand signs that she should watch the center hall while he stood close to the door and wrapped his hand around the glass knob.

And when it turned, she wanted to run.

Suddenly, there was ice on the floor, ice in the air, and she pressed a trembling hand against her chest, feeling the light chain that hung there and the ring that dangled between her breasts. It had been Marc's idea to wear it. Protection. Against . . . something.

He hissed and she spun around, saw him vanish into the room. Quickly, she patted the ring for luck, and followed.

"No," she said, relieved and disappointed. "It's not the same place. It must be the one next door."

The room was smaller than the others she'd seen, tastefully appointed with oriental throws, massive armchairs and a writing desk set against one wall. There was a fireplace opposite them, lighted to cast wavering shadows on a small divan, a marble-topped coffee table, and a wing chair embroidered black against wine. There were no other lights but the flames.

A waiting room, she thought, searching for a connecting door leading to something like a bedroom or bath. And as her eyes adjusted to the changing light, she found it between two life-sized portraits of Ambrose Toal.

"Well," Marc said without moving. "Ambrose in riding breeches, Ambrose in aspic. Nice."

"Thank you," Toal said, and Natalie instantly grabbed for Marc's arm and pulled herself close. The wing chair suddenly sprouted a head, and Toal twisted around to beckon them. "Come over and sit with me. I won't bite you."

Natalie shook her head, but followed Marc to the divan as Toal maneuvered the chair so he would be facing them when they sat. He was dressed in a Mandarin's gown unembossed except for the familiar ring design in the center of his chest. His feet were bare, and his hair was wetly dark and close to his skull. On his left hand was the ring.

A feeling that she should be cowering was dismissed as she rallied in the belief that somehow she was at least momentarily in possession of the advantage. It was a temporary meeting of equals, and would remain so as long as she kept the security of the book and Ben's ring.

Toal casually lighted a cigarette from a taper he pulled from the fire. Then he pointed to Natalie's ankh. "Is that supposed to ward off the Devil, Mrs. Windsor?"

"You're still sitting there, aren't you?" she said.

He laughed and applauded once. "Oh, bravo, Mrs. Windsor! You have an astute mind. And courageous. An admirable quality so little found in this day and age. Now," and he held out a hand, "the book, if you please."

She applauded back, mockingly. "Bravo, yourself, Mr. Toal. But I'll see you in hell first."

"She could have said shove it," Marc muttered, "but she's too much of a lady."

Toal barely maintained his jovial expression, and the obvious strain made Natalie think there was hope after all. She shifted until her back was flush against the cushions. Then she crossed her legs and pushed her hood back to her shoulders, shaking her head to free the auburn hair she knew was glinting sparks from the light of the fire.

"You owe me an explanation," she said flatly.

Toal considered it, looked to Marc who had moved to the corner and had his arm laid across the back of the divan. Then he nodded. "Yes, I suppose I do at that." He tented his fingers and rested his chin delicately on their tips. "It began—"

"History I don't need, nor do I want it, Mr. Toal," Natalie said quickly, sensing a stall. "Just tell me what's going on. Why are you trying to kill me?"

"And keep me from getting back into town," Marc said, his disgust undisguised.

"Ah, two against one. Unfair, Mrs. Windsor." He shrugged as though his case was hopeless. "But it will be as you say. For now." He smiled. "Your late husband, Ben, was an important man to us, you see. Had he lived, in fact, he probably would have taken my place here. But," and the full sleeves spread wide, "he fell in love with you, and he knew you would never agree with our little plan. In failing that, and in refusing to see that you were permanently removed from his area of conflict, he had to be removed. A necessity, you see, or he might have said things to you that would hardly be to our advantage. It's a good thing you thought his ring was silly, Mrs. Windsor. A good thing."

She nodded understanding, hiding her dismay and surging guilt feelings.

"It has always been my contention, you see," the financier continued, "that there are ways and there are ways to get people to do what you want. You can browbeat them, impress them with their own inferiority, threaten them with physical harm. But in the long run nothing like that ever works because, in the long run, you are never in final command. You are mortal, you see, and as you age you lose the vitality you had as a youth." He turned to Marc. "That's why I was so disappointed in those so-called money emperors, Mr. Clayton."

"Thanks for getting my name right for a change," Marc said, and Natalie stifled a grin.

"They wasted too much energy on the useless things, not enough in seeking out those things that truly count."

"Like the ring?" Natalie said.

Toal looked as though he'd been slapped, but his recovery was rapid. "No. Not quite, Mrs. Windsor. More exactly, what the ring represents."

"Satan?"

"Absolutely not!" He leaned forward, his arms resting on his thighs. "But it is true that there are worlds outside our own. I knew it had to be because otherwise there would be no gods, no demons, no legends of superhuman heroes. There had to be something, the fire in the smoke, and once I had convinced myself of that, I was determined to discover what it was, harness it if I could, and make my little fortune, if you will."

" 'To direct the Eye, open the Lid,' " Natalie quoted softly.

"Well," Toal said with a shade of displeasure, "I see you have read my guardian tome. Yes, for want of a better direction, I call the way to this other world the Eye, and in order to see you have to lift your eyelid, don't you?"

"And what did you see?" Marc asked, fascination in his voice despite the danger he was in.

"I have no word for it," Toal answered angrily. "There is no word for it. Labels are confining, but it is a place of living things . . . energy organisms, if you will, that lie unformed and undirected. Mediums and psychics tap it when they fall into trances. Their own minds shape this energy and they mistakenly label it visitors from beyond the grave, beyond the plane, and all the other tripe they create in their ignorance. I, however," and he tapped his chest for emphasis, "recognize it for what it is, a source of control and immortality that need only be exercised as one would a disused muscle before one can successfully manipulate . . ." and he spread his arms wide again, "anything."

"And the rings?" Natalie said.

"Conductors, perhaps, and insulation. To tap this world of mine is a dangerous process for the uninitiated, Mrs. Windsor, and fatal for the unprotected. Simple. I made them myself."

That he believed what he was saying was frightening enough, but that what he was saying also pieced together the puzzle confused and terrified her.

"It's this energy, then," Marc was saying, "that keeps me from Oxrun when I leave. You can't control me directly for some reason, so you hide from me just as you hide from the rest of the world."

"Well, I wouldn't say hide from you, Mr. Clayton, but you do have the general principle. I extend, let's say, a veil of control over the Station, and the workings of the minds that inhabit it so they can find their way back. All the little people, Mr. Clayton, are essential, or the mechanics of the community would grind to a halt. Those minds I can't control, I eliminate."

"The books," Natalie said, revulsion welling in her throat. "What about the books?"

Toal lighted another cigarette, and his face took on an expression of tragic sorrow. "Mrs. Windsor, every dictator since the dawn of man knows it will not do to have his subjects think too much along the wrong lines. Those books that would have aided them were replaced. They had to be, or somebody might have tumbled too soon."

She couldn't ignore the feeling any longer. "You are a murderer."

"I protect myself, Mrs. Windsor," Toal said haughtily. "When I have perfected the Oxrun control, I will be able to step outward." He rose and stared into the fire. "It won't be an easy thing, but I will do it. You have seen what I can do, not only for myself but to others." He turned, and the gown was a shimmering emptiness ringed by flame. "I literally have all the time in the world, Mrs. Windsor. It has taken me over a century to get this far. What's another two or three when the end is plainly in sight. I come to the final act, Mrs. Windsor. Tonight I will create a permanent breach in the wall to my world, and when it happens, when all that decadent energy downstairs is added to the power you'll find up here, I'll have everything I need to shape my control." His hand lifted to the design, stretched outward. "The ring, Mrs. Windsor. The party has ended."

Natalie shook her head quickly, but couldn't stop her hand from jumping to her chest. Toal uttered a choking exclamation and darted forward as she twisted away over the divan's arm. Marc leaped to his feet and kicked the coffee table into Toal's legs, causing him to spill over it.

Natalie backed to the door, then, while Marc fell onto the millionaire's back and began pummeling his head and shoulders until Toal stopped squirming. He slumped, one fist raised, then turned around. His grin faded instantly and his eyes widened.

"Natalie, behind—"

She spun too late. Hands gripped her shoulders and pinned her arms to her side. She was lifted bodily off the floor and her backward kicks were ineffectual and ultimately painful as the wooden sandals dropped from her feet and clattered against the wall.

And as she struggled, too angry to scream, she saw Marc rise, take a step over Toal's body, then fall hard as though he'd been clubbed. Behind him, a dark figure in front of the fire smiled and dropped the poker onto the chair.

There was pressure on the back of her neck, a sharp pain that stiffened her spine, and the room went black.

Seconds later she regained consciousness and realized she was being carried on Sam's shoulder through the door between the portraits. Marc was being dragged ahead of them, Artemus Hall clutching his heels, ignoring the thumping Marc's head was receiving.

And they were in the room Natalie had seen the night she had fled from Toal's women.

They were placed, then, on the outer rim of the floor, facing the center and the light, which had been replaced by a kerosene cousin flickering at the end off the black linked chain. Figures were sitting in a tight circle on the ebony floor directly under the flame. All of them were naked.

She recognized without triumph the Halls, the Bains, Elaine and Sam, Dederson, two school officials, Wayne, Bradford the jeweler, and Karl Hampton. None turned to acknowledge her, none bothered to look at her when she pulled her legs beneath her and crawled over to Marc. She bit back a sob and cradled his head in her lap, brushing tenderly at the dark-matted hair where the poker had split his scalp. He would die if she didn't get him medical aid soon, and there was no help to be had in this diabolical room. Her eyes wide, she tried to see beyond the reach of the light, searching for the door through which she'd been carried, or the door she knew led into the hall. But the velvet hangings were complete, and a reconnaissance would easily be intercepted. She bent over, then, and kissed his forehead, rocking slowly and trying with the hem of her sleeve to stem the flow of blood from his wound.

A cold wind. The light swayed, and the shadows moved as if they were alive.

Silence was complete.

Cynthia, naked except for a loin cloth of silver, and red paint on her nipples, stepped out of the darkness and stood on the far side of the circle.

Christine, totally naked, moved to the circle's center and lifted her arms to the light. The ring on her hand flashed red and silver, and the others began a swaying soft motion in perfect time.

And finally, after what seemed like a century, there was Ambrose, still robed, parting the increasingly frigid air to stand by her side. His hand reached down and she stared up at him dumbly.

"The book," he said, and she refused. "The book!" he repeated, and his voice was the void on the other side of midnight. "You can't use it, Mrs. Windsor." The hand moved to poise itself over Marc's throat. "Give it to me, Mrs. Windsor, or I'll kill him now!"

A weight made its presence at the back of her neck, making her slump forward, ease Marc's head off her lap. She groped under his toga, unfastened the strap and pulled out the book. Her arm was a leaden bar when she lifted it, heavier still when he took the volume and carried it to the floor.

And there was only the sound of his bare feet on the wood, the slide of buttocks as the circle expanded to give double-arms' distance to each of the disciples. Christine backed away from the center and Toal was in her place. She stood, then, beside her daughter, and they joined hands in reaching for the light whose pendulum motion now carried it parallel to the floor.

Natalie closed her eyes tightly as she was forced prone, fighting the sensation that a block of marble was crushing her bones into the wood.

She felt it, then: a tingling that made the

hairs on her neck stand, her longer hair fly out from her head. The caftan snapped to cling warmly to her skin, and her teeth began to ache.

The light swung faster, its passage the only sound in the room: a swift, loud and soft hissing.

Like the blade of a sword whipped over her head.

Fists were raised and, with an anguished twist of her head, she saw the rings snaring the glow, turning the red to scarlet, the scarlet to crimson, and through it all a lightning flash of white-bright silver.

They are calling it, she thought suddenly. This is how they do it. Toal can't do it alone; and the revelation of his empty boasts buoyed her, gave her the strength to push herself up to her elbows.

The only face clearly visible now was his, upraised, stone, the ring positioned in front of his eyes that were wide and staring as though the madness of the look alone could conjure the forces he claimed to control.

Darts of light from the eyes of the rings reached out and clashed, mingled, and spread again until they met, separated, met yet once more. A web of slender red interwoven with snakes of silver.

Toal moved his hand, and the web converged on his ring. The electricity increased, the cold made her teeth chatter, yet the backs of the people nearest her were running with perspiration.

The final act, Mrs. Windsor. Tonight I will create a permanent breach in that wall to my world, and when it happens ... I'll have everything I need to shape my control.

Suddenly, she felt a tugging at her chest. She looked down and saw a bulge under the cloth. She slapped at it, but it refused to lie flat. She looked up again, and Toal was beginning to strain. His arms trembled, and the web wavered slightly.

Natalie wanted to shout to shatter his concentration, but though her mouth opened, there was no sound but the hiss of the light.

She tried to pound her fist on the floor, but she could not find the strength to do more than a feeble tap.

And Toal's chest was heaving. A lack she sensed he might overcome and succeed; the web steadied, shimmered, steadied once again.

The bulging distracted her, and she watched as the ankh pendant slid sideways, felt the wool press tight across her back. Her neck was pulled forward, and elation demanded a scream of discovery. As rapidly as the lack of room would allow, she hiked up her robe and grabbed at the ring, yanked and cried out silently as the chain dug into her skin. It was Ben's ring he was missing, what he needed to make the transition as simple, as easy as always. He might be able to do without its intersection into the web, but its destruction would ...

Hooking a finger through it to keep it with

her, she placed the thin band on the floor, raised a fist, and held it in the air as its rubies began to pulse, its silver stroke glimmered and strained upward. No! she thought, I'll not be his damned key after all this! She struck it, felt it bite into her flesh, but though it was fragile, it was still too much for her bare hands to damage. She reached down to her feet.

The light swayed, its hissing climbing to a thundering roar.

Toal began to smile, his lips twisted ferally.

Natalie groped flesh; the wooden sandals had fallen while she'd struggled.

The roaring pitched to a catlike snarling, and there were images in the air, in and through and above the sun-bright web. Sparks of colors that had no name. Gathering, spiraling, whirling above Toal's head.

Natalie clutched frantically at her temples, pounded them, forcing the encroaching dizziness to retreat. She twisted and felt a weight at her breasts, reached up and grabbed the heavy ankh. Licking her lips. Falling to her face. The ring not an inch from her eyes, strands of crimson writhing slowly into the air.

She bent her head and slid the braided necklace free, but the ankh as a tool was a feeble, frustrating failure until she realized she would have to use the room to defeat itself.

Snarling to screeching.

The images solidifying.

The ring, and Toal's eyes.

Feeling her muscles tearing, knowing at least one small bone in her wrist had snapped under the strain, she lifted her arm until the elbow locked. Pressure beginning to break through her skull. Painfully, blood seeping down her arm, dripping onto the floor, her fingers maneuvered the ankh until it was held like a dagger; the blood made it slippery, and she waited no longer but let the weight of Toal's world thrust her arm, her hand, the edge of the ankh down upon her finger, and the rim of the ring.

She saw it split, shatter, rise into sparks that died in the cold wind. Saw her finger severed, saw the ankh embedded in the black floor.

The silence of the moment ended, and she heard a grumbling that mushroomed into a lightless explosion while a man screamed and screamed and screamed above the roaring.

She saw the swaying chain snap and the lantern shatter against the far wall. Flames of no color spread up the velvet and became orange and blue and a licking deep gold that rushed in a living river toward the figures in the middle of the floor.

The weight lifted. Vanished. Left her gulping the cold air.

The screaming continued, augmented by others joining rage with terror, fury with hate.

There was light again, wavering. The room flamed into a furnace, and Natalie heard herself cry out, calling Marc's name and seeing him stir. Without thought, she jammed her hands under his shoulders and pulled him to the near wall, felt the flesh of her fingers peel away as she yanked at the velvet and, in its falling, exposed the hall door. It opened, and she and Marc and the fire spilled into the corridor.

The agony of her maimed hand numbed her senses one by one.

As she heard a man scream, a guest walking by, caught in the consuming fire tide that attacked the rugs and the drapes opposite.

As she smelled the charred stench of blackening flesh.

As she tasted the blood of the hand at her mouth.

As she felt the stub where her finger had been.

As she saw through the flames in the holocaust room.

Saw Toal glaring at her, his ring impotent before him.

Saw at his throat the fangs of a cat tearing, ripping, shredding his flesh and scattering its blood until the flames closed round and the ceiling collapsed.

A hand at her back and someone lifted her. She called out for Marc and watched as a Satan cradled him and raced down the hall.

There was pain, and she screamed until she fainted.

There was pain, numbing, and she slept beneath cool sheets.

There was pain, faded, and when she opened her eyes, Marc was sitting on the edge of the bed. His head was swathed in clean-smelling bandages, and his hands were covered by thick white gloves.

But he was smiling as he lay a hand to her cheek.

"This," he said, "is getting to be a habit."

THE BEST IN HORROR

JOHN FARRIS

"America's premier novelist of terror. When he turns it on, nobody does it better."   —Stephen King

"Farris is a giant of contemporary horror!"
                                        —Peter Straub

Ramsey Campbell

☐ 51652-4   DARK COMPANIONS $3.50
    51653-2   Canada $3.95

☐ 51654-0   THE DOLL WHO ATE HIS $3.50
    51655-9   MOTHER   Canada $3.95

☐ 51658-3   THE FACE THAT MUST DIE $3.95
    51659-1   Canada $4.95

☐ 51650-8   INCARNATE $3.95
    51651-6   Canada $4.50

☐ 58125-3   THE NAMELESS $3.50
    58126-1   Canada $3.95

☐ 51656-7   OBSESSION $3.95
    51657-5   Canada $4.95

Buy them at your local bookstore or use this handy coupon:
Clip and mail this page with your order

TOR BOOKS—Reader Service Dept.
49 W. 24 Street 9th Floor, New York, NY 10010

Please send me the book(s) I have checked above. I am enclosing
$_____ (please add $1.00 to cover postage and handling).
Send check or money order only—no cash or C.O.D.'s.

Mr./Mrs./Miss _____

Address _____

City _____ State/Zip _____

Please allow six weeks for delivery. Prices subject to change
without notice.

GRAHAM MASTERTON

☐ 52195-1 CONDOR $3.50
      52196-X   Canada $3.95

☐ 52191-9 IKON $3.95
      52192-7   Canada $4.50

☐ 52193-5 THE PARIAH $3.50
      52194-3   Canada $3.95

☐ 52189-7 SOLITAIRE $3.95
      52190-0   Canada $4.50

☐ 48067-9 THE SPHINX $2.95

☐ 48061-X TENGU $3.50

☐ 48042-3 THE WELLS OF HELL $2.95

☐ 52199-4 PICTURE OF EVIL $3.95
      52200-1   Canada $4.95